KANE 4

King Coopa J

KANE 4

Available on Amazon

Atlanta: Dope Boyz In The Trap

Lifted: Power Money and Speed

Matt Cain: The Hero

Kane

Kane 2

Kane 3

32 Points

Upcoming Titles

You Killed Mama (Matt Cain)

The Japanese Messenger

Kane 5

Atlanta 2

1 – General

The General looked around his office, pondering his next move on the rebels. The rebel army had caused more problems within his smuggling business as of late. While he was out of the country trying to secure the African Black Diamond as his brother, also the South African president, had commanded. The rebels had raided his military artillery camps, taking whatever they could grab. He didn't receive any of the money promised from his brother because he'd failed to bring home the diamond. His next move had to be great, or the president would have his head put on a stake.

The General watched people move about through his massive office window. He heard a knock at the door. He didn't bother walking over to ask who was interrupting his time of peace. "It's open, lieutenant." He continued to face the outside world. His mind moved to another place after the death of his father. The diamond was the cause of his murder, and the

1

General would do anything to retrieve the precious stone, even if it meant going against his brother's rule.

"General," the lieutenant stepped into the office. "My apologies for interrupting. I've come to ask how you wish to proceed with the rebels?"

It was a question that he couldn't avoid with everything that had happened up until this point. Mainly with his brother putting an end to their field supplies. The army needed more weapons to deal with the rebels. He didn't have enough guns to supply all of his men. If he decided to move forward and attack the rebels, some would attend the battle without a weapon to fire. Instead, they would have to make use of knives, grenades, spears, or whatever they could construct to defend themselves. His army outnumbered the rebels, but the outcome would be intensely felt due to the number of casualties they would suffer in a war with another country. If only he had a replacement for Bill Right, the man he knew as Jar Simmons.

"How would you like us to deal with the situation, Abrafo?" The General asked his most trusted comrade. For years, they had known each other since they were kids, training to become soldiers in the African military. The General excelled in war strategy while Abrafo exceeded in kills. And that's what his name stands for . . . executioner. The General gave Abrafo his name after learning about his family history. They were

2

assassins, and the name Abrafo suited him well. It was the General's way of protecting his only friend's identity.

"You are our leader," Lieutenant Abrafo replied. "It would be wise for you to give the command, not me. I am a man of war, and you are a man of approach. Your tactic will be far more effective than mine."

The General turned from the window to face Abrafo. "Do you think it would be wise to start a war with the rebels?" The General wanted to test the lieutenant to see his view of their unfortunate circumstance.

It didn't take long for Abrafo to understand what the General asked of him. The General wouldn't ask a third time for his opinion. "No, General." The answer was short, the way he intended for it to be, knowing a *why* question would follow.

"Why do you feel as such?" The General asked curiously. Abrafo didn't become a high-ranking lieutenant by being a cretinous man. The army had to confront the rebels from a different standpoint, and the General needed a fresh perspective. Abrafo was more than a killer to him. He would be the General's new plan of action until his mind was off the diamond. He couldn't lead his men into a war without a clear sense of reason.

"The rebels are growing strong in numbers," the lieutenant said evenly. "And they're confident now that they have successfully raided our camps for weapons. We will lose more soldiers than intended if we face them without first breaking their spirit."

"Break their spirit," the General folded his hands behind his back. "And how would you suggest proceeding without a battle?"

The lieutenant took a short moment to think about an answer. If he replied quickly, the General would possibly void his response. He looked to be deep in thought. His explanation had to be clear of mistakes and thoughtful. He spoke when formulating the right choice of words. "The same way you stop a fire-breathing dragon."

The General smiled at Abrafo. "We cut off the head."

Abrafo balled his first and placed it over his heart. "For Africa."

The General followed suit. "For Africa."

2 – Kane

"How much longer," Smoke sounded from the seat across from mine. "It's been hours, and my legs feel paralyzed."

I looked back at my friend and smiled. Honestly, I was happy he could move his legs at all. Adrian had shot him in the leg, and Smoke had to use a cane to stand up straight for a week. At first, I thought he would never be the same, but that was just me worrying too much. My guy pulled through just fine.

"It's not that bad," Kim said. "We'll get there in the next thirty minutes or so. Sit back and relax, crybaby."

Smoke threw his head back on the seat rest, frustrated.

I shook my head and turned my attention back to the map I had picked up in a store at the airport. We were on our way to Africa. Even Big Bruce decided to come with us. I told him it could get ugly, and he was still down to ride. None of us were in trouble with the law, so I booked a commercial flight straight to Tripoli, Libya. It cost me $1500 a ticket. Not that it mattered, but damn, I know now why people save money for vacations. This was my first time leaving the country, and it felt good to get away even though I was traveling to find my mother.

I didn't have my father's black notebook anymore. It would've been helpful because it had names and locations. The only thing I had to lean on was the map in my father's office. There were pinned locations that corresponded with the notebook. That's how I figured out my mother would be somewhere in Libya. It's where my father built his organization and headquarters. Where I assume he stored the money and weapons. The only thing I couldn't figure out was why my mother chose Jordan over me? We could've done this together.

"How long are you gonna stare at that map?" Kim asked. "What are you trying to figure out that we don't know already?"

"Roads, places," I gave her a short answer. "Studying the landscape."

"Why," she asked and leaned her head against my shoulder.

"One, I think it'd be best if I at least know where we're at," I informed her. "And two, I'm searching for an unoccupied area away from the city. Somewhere, a plane can land without being noticed by the army."

"I thought your father worked with the army?"

I looked around and saw several people staring at us. Mostly Africans, heading back to their homeland after visiting America.

After Kim said, *your father worked with the army*, we caught ugly glares from everyone who heard. "Keep your voice down," I whispered. "I don't think foreigners should be talking about the army."

She secretly looked around and spotted the people with hard eyes on us. "Right."

"Anyway," I began. "I wasn't talking about Libya's army. I was talking about rebel armies who'd love to get their hands on money and weapons. My father would've avoided those areas to prevent any problems."

"What if he paid them off," she remembered to speak with a low voice.

"It's possible," I said. "But why spend extra money when you can just stay off the grid?" My father wouldn't work with them knowing they were against the army—too much of a headache."

"For you," she replied.

"I think like him," I smiled.

"Whatever, smart guy," she kissed my cheek.

I believe it to be true that my father wouldn't work with a malicious group. The notebook had names of Generals and prominent figures written in it. He was larger than life, and it would take more than a few soldiers to protect what he built. He used to tell me, don't work hard at something if you're gonna half-ass in the end? I wouldn't do it, so why would he? The only

7

thing I ever smuggled was contraband from one cell to another when I was locked up. The guards didn't allow inmates to trade anything, so we had to move low-key. I met a guy who would watch my cell while I was on free time for a pack of cigarettes a week. Inmates would sneak into your cell and steal goods while you were away watching TV or occupied in the yard. After it happened to me once, I knew that I had to hire help. I paid a killer to watch over other inmates with sticky fingers, and it worked. This situation was no different. My father hired the army so he could move freely on the land, but that didn't mean the rebels wouldn't try their hand. If you build a restaurant around rats, they'll eat your food. That's how I look at it. And . . . there are plenty of rats where we're going, if you know what I mean.

3 – Abel

Abel checked his watch and smiled. Silva had successfully landed the plane in Africa. They had touchdown just past the border of Mali. Abel looked around the area through the side window and saw the desert go on for miles. The sand and dirt covering the area appeared to be endless, and he had already begun to feel the heat beaming down from the sun. He stood when the plane came to a complete stop, opting to sit in the back to keep a close eye on Silva and Britt.

"How hot is it?" Gina stood and wiped the sweat from her forehead. The heat made her want to ask Silva to fly them back home. She had never experienced a high temperature at this level, and it was more than enough to get her frustrated.

"It's one hundred and five degrees," Snake answered exasperatedly.

"What the fuck," Gina muttered at nobody in particular.

"I'm getting woozy," Bam stood and dropped back into the seat. "I don't know if I can do this. It's too hot for me to think straight."

Gina formed a disgusted expression on her face when she looked at Bam. It was her moment to comment on his weakness, but receiving a response would've gotten her even angrier in combination with the sun. The heat provided her enough irritation to deal with for now.

"Get yourself together," Abel told Bam before opening the plane's side door. He immediately felt a strong breeze of heat attack his entire body as if an unknown entity forced it. The fury of wind lasted a short span before he was able to step off the aircraft. Abel held up his hand and spotted a large dome tent and a 4x4 off-road jeep. The campsite appeared invisible from the air. It was the perfect color for someone who wished to camouflage it with the surrounding landscape.

Silva turned off the engine and followed the others off the plane. He stood next to Abel and pointed at the dome tent. "Dat a ih."

Mali was the closest destination Silva could land without the army noticing the aircraft. Abel knew this to be true with the amount of illegal activity that had taken place throughout the years. If he desired a safe and secure landing, Mali was the only option without the plane getting shot down. He turned to Bam and Snake. "Unload the supplies."

Bam spoke up, "What about her?" his eyes were on Gina, wondering why Abel didn't ask her to help.

"Shut up, you idiot," Snake eyed Bam.

Abel didn't bother to turn around when he spoke. "I want you to be alive when I return."

Bam was mind-boggled with Abel's response. His words rang out in his mind . . . *I want you to be alive when I return.* Bam planned to murder Gina before leaving America, and he knew that she carried the same intentions. Abel was right. They couldn't be left alone together, not even for a second. He sucked his teeth and followed Snake back inside the plane.

Gina smirked at Bam as he turned away, thinking his time would come. *Keep on, tough guy,* she thought. Hiding her anger toward Bam was becoming a daily task. When Abel no longer needs Bam, he's dead. He was at the top of her to-kill list, without a doubt.

Britt stepped beside Abel. "I noticed you're in pain while on the plane. Is everything alright with you?" She had a concerned look on her face.

Gina bumped Britt out of her way and stood next to Abel. "He's fine," she snarled. "Let's go inside. It's fucking hot out here." She held Abel's arm and guided him toward the tent.

11

Silva witnessed the tension between Gina and Britt. He was still unaware of how Britt felt about Abel. She hadn't shown any signs of feelings for him until now. "Blurtnawt," he muttered, walking past Britt.

Abel stopped at the tent's door, waiting for Silva to catch up and lead the way inside. "After you," he smiled at Silva as if opening the door would spring a trap.

"Yah mon," Silva pulled back the opening, showing there was nothing to fear. After stepping inside, he called to the man sitting Indian-style on a throw rug in front of them. "Oyoo."

Oyoo opened his eyes and stared at them. He had a mean expression on his face as though they disrupted his concentration while meditating. After a short moment of studying the other unknown guests, he smiled at his friend. "Silva," Oyoo sounded excited and stood to greet him.

Abel stood firm by the door with Gina as the two men shook hands. He kept his eyes on Oyoo the entire time while on high alert. If he missed any potential threats, Gina would take care of it. That's why he wanted her to come inside with him. Her awareness was greater than Bam and Snake's put together, which kept him at ease.

Oyoo looked over Silva's shoulder and spoke. "That man reminds me of someone. Who is he?"

Silva turned around and faced Abel. "Di dead mon son."

12

Oyoo's eyes widened. "Jar," he said in shock. He stepped closer to Abel. "Have you come to take his place?" Oyoo noticed Abel's muscular physique, and the man was by far larger than his father. Oyoo worked with Jar for more than twenty years as a driver. When beginning the smuggling business, Silva and Oyoo were Jar's first transportation hires. Jar cared for them to the point that there wasn't a need to work for anyone else. Even after Jar's death, the men were well off, but they loved making money and stayed in business as contractors for anyone looking to transport.

Abel scanned Oyoo as he approached, noticing he was a man of the land who could speak perfect English. He was surprised by that and how well kept it was inside the tent. He expected it to be dusty and hot. It was neither, and somehow the sun rays didn't affect the inside temperature. "I haven't decided as of yet."

"Then why have you come, son of Jar?" Oyoo looked at Abel's chest and felt his pain. It was a gift he possessed that allowed him to sense the aura surrounding the body.

"I've come for the General," Abel answered truthfully. "I have a gift for him."

Oyoo smiled sarcastically. "A gift for the General. The man who brings war to his people." Oyoo turned away from Abel. "What gift do you bring, if not weapons? He values his army,

13

and your father made a business of it. Your gift will get you killed."

"I beg to differ," Abel said confidently. "I have something he's been searching for."

Oyoo turned around and thought, *could he possibly have it?* There was only one thing the General would accept besides weapons. And that would be the African Black Diamond. He was well aware of the rebels raiding the campsites. The General announced that anyone who worked with the rebels would be killed. "You have it?"

Abel signed with a slight nod.

"Okay, I will lead you to the General, but I will not reveal myself," Oyoo said, hiding his true intentions. He pointed to Abel's chest. "I will show you to a doctor before we go. You will need all of your strength, son of Jar."

4 – Jordan

Noti looked at the surrounding area and noticed a plane at their landing spot. It's been several years since she returned to the landing zone. It was one of many locations Jar used for travel. She remembered meeting Oyoo with her husband at a bar in Bamako. Oyoo worked as a tour guide and offered to show them around the city. Jar accepted, and the next day Oyoo picked them up from a hotel. They toured the entire town, and Jar was impressed with Oyoo's sense of direction and driving skills. It was enough for Jar to extend a proposal for Oyoo to be part of the business.

Noti thought about landing the plane anyway but quickly decided it wouldn't be a good idea. Her husband was dead, and she figured Oyoo had found a new boss. Nobody knew who she was except Oyoo, and whoever it was visiting might not be friendly. They were in dangerous waters, and steering clear of violence was the key to staying alive a day longer. "We need to land at another location."

"I thought this was the location," Adrian spoke up from the pilot's seat. "I don't see anywhere else to land."

Rick sat in the back of the plane next to Jordan. He'd never been more terrified in his life. Jordan and his brother Adrian were monsters. After Jordan woke up, he became himself again, and the FBI agent was gone. He lashed out at Adrian for knocking him over the head. Adrian could've wrecked the plane if Noti and Rick didn't stop him in time. Jordan kept his eyes on his brother for most of the trip. Rick thought if he closed his eyes for a second, they all be dead. Sleep was not an option either, and he damn near didn't blink.

"Land this fucking plane," Jordan growled at Adrian. "You said this was the spot, and now you've changed your mind all of a sudden. That's not gonna work for me. This flight is over." He stared at Noti hard. She somehow became the bandleader, which didn't sit right with him. She'd be useless if he could get her to give up the safe location and the passcode. Striking that kind of luck would end her life, and he knew it wouldn't happen. He'd never get the information, not if she desired to live. Jordan's frustration dictated his actions, and until he regained control of the situation, his goal was to piss them off.

"Never mind the plane," Noti said evenly. "And prepare yourself for a fight. That's the only option if we land now."

"She's right," Rick spoke up. He noticed the aircraft and spotted two men unloading luggage.

"Well, we have to land soon," Adrian checked the gasoline level meter. "We're running short on fuel." They had to miss a fuel station because a police boat docked nearby. He couldn't risk it and let the last opportunity pass by.

Jordan began to spaz out, letting his emotion run wild. "Fuck!" he roared and started to destroy anything in reach. "How are we runnin' short on fuel?" He tossed random items to the front of the plane. He picked up a glass of water and threw it at the front window, just missing Adrian. "Goddammit!"

"Someone calm his ass down," Adrian shouted and took a split second to glance back at Jordan. That would've been the last straw if the glass hit him. Jordan was pushing it to the maximum limit, and Adrian was more than ready to do something harmful to his brother, even if it meant ending his arrangement with Noti.

Rick turned his attention from the plane below and focused on his former partner. "Shit," he muttered and tried to defuse Jordan's outrage. He held up his hands and blocked Jordan from throwing more items toward the cockpit. "Are you trying to kill us?"

"Get the hell out of my way, Rick." Jordan had the devil inside of him and wasn't afraid to show it. The Planner was the cause of his outrage. It wasn't his fault the plane was running out of fuel. It wasn't his fault Noti was the one in control. It wasn't his fault Rick had to tag along with them. So many different things began to fester inside his head, and he wanted to break loose. Freeing himself from everyone and unleashing his anger was the only way to do it. It made him feel good, and Rick kept trying to stop that sensation.

"I can't let you distract your brother from landing this plane safely." Rick kept his hands up and continued to block Jordan's path. *Why did I get myself into this,* he thought. He wouldn't be in this predicament if he only called for backup when discovering the cabin. Obey the rules as an officer and follow protocol. That's all it takes, and he failed to do both when Adrian apprehended him in the woods.

Jordan suddenly felt exhausted, and he just stood there, staring at Rick like a madman. His chest heaved in and out, taking in deep breaths of air. He needed water before he passed out from dehydration. It was hot, and his energy output didn't agree with the heat from the sun. He looked at the cooler on the side of the seat. Hopefully, there was another bottle of water inside. He reached for it, and Rick reacted by moving in his way. "Get the hell out of my way. I need a drink."

18

Rick sighed and looked at the cooler. "Okay," he moved to the side.

Jordan opened the cooler and cracked open a water bottle. He tossed the cap at Rick's chest, and it bounced off to the ground. He smirked at him, "Rookie."

The whole time Jordan was having a fit, Noti focused on the plane below. The men appeared to be Americans. Maybe they were smugglers who prospered after her husband's death. When a king is dead, a new one will rise in any case. The luggage couldn't carry the number of weapons it takes to feed one rebel group. There could be a second plane, or money was in the bags. Suddenly, a woman and Oyoo emerged from the tent. Her eyes were sharp enough to assure it was him. She learned to see from a flying distance in the beginning stages of Jar's operation. He wasn't the only one taking risks for their future. *It can't be,* she thought.

Another figure emerged from the dome tent. Noti was stunned after realizing a demon had followed her to Africa. As the plane passed over the location, she could've sworn Abel looked into the aircraft and made eye contact with her. She fell back from the window in shock. Her heart rate began to speed up a notch, and she felt like it would explode. Abel could have caused her to have a mild heart attack. She put her hand over her chest in fear.

19

Rick caught her from falling to the ground before speaking to her worriedly. "Are you okay?"

"No," she answered seriously. "The devil has arrived."

5 – Kane

The plane finally landed, and a woman flight attendant spoke to us through the intercom. "Welcome to Tripoli, Libya," she began and went through safety precautions before we could exit the aircraft.

Smoke was the first to stand up. "Thank God that's over!" he grabbed his bag from the top compartment and strapped it around his shoulders. "Y'all ready?"

"Damn, bruh," Bruce spoke up. "Give us a chance to get up."

"I just did," Smoke gave him a look that said, try me.

Bruce stared back into Smoke's eyes for a moment, then sighed. "Whatever, nigga."

I eyed them and shook my head while laughing on the inside. Even though Bruce played his part back at the police impound by helping us escape, he and Smoke still went at each other every now and then. Bruce proved to us that he could be trusted to a small degree, but that bit of trust only ever so slightly moved the needle for Smoke. I was cool with it because I didn't expect them to be all buddy, buddy. Hell, the smart remarks they made at each other were funny to me. At least they weren't trying to kill one another.

"Somebody, please wake up, Bear," Kim whined. "I don't have the time or patience." She unlocked the compartment above us, grabbed a Chanel backpack, and strapped it around her shoulders.

"On it," I looked at Bear and thought this man was crazy. His arms were locked around a Gucci backpack that he failed to put away. As soon as we got on the airplane, he sat down and fell asleep for the entire trip. I don't think he even got up to use the restroom. Bear doesn't snore, so I guess we all were lucky.

I got my bag down and unzipped it, looking for a particular item I had brought for this special occasion. I figured Bear would pass out on us. I couldn't wake him up the usual way by screaming in his ear or slappin' the dog shit out of him while on the plane. Those tactics would probably cause a stir. I came up with another idea that I tested before the trip, and it worked two out of the three times I tried it. Those odds were good enough for me. I found what I was looking for. It was a polyester swab with a thin six-inch handle. I looked around to ensure no one outside the crew was watching me. When it was clear, I moved in.

22

"What the hell are you doing?" Bruce asked skeptically.

"Wait and see, big dawg." I took the swab and stuck it in Bear's nose, slowly moving it deeper until it was far enough to make him react. I swiftly retracted the swab from his nostril when I felt he was about to move.

Bear's body twitched as if he got shot, but he never let go of his bag. "What the," he opened his eyes and looked around, scared. It was the only time you'd ever see that type of expression on his face.

A big grin spread across my face as I watched him stare into my eyes. "Welcome back, big dawg."

Bruce began to laugh, "You wrong as hell for that one."

"Bruh," Smoke had a stunned look on his face.

Kim popped the back of my head, "Don't ever let me see you do that again." She looked at Bear, concerned. "You good?"

Bear got up, "I'm straight." He strapped his bag around his shoulders and looked at me. "Imma fuck you up."

I put my hand on his shoulder, "Stop crying."

Bear looked behind me and saw Smoke and Bruce chuckling, "Y'all niggas." He turned around and followed Kim off the plane.

We got our luggage and made our way through the Mitiga International Airport. We didn't carry much with us. We each brought a backpack and suitcase, that's it. The airport was no different from ours in America. The only difference was the people, and mainly, the military presence. There were soldiers stationed throughout the building. At every turn, a soldier would be on guard. They didn't give us any problems, but the fact that they were around, scared me. Why they were there was the first thing that came to mind? It could be they're watching out for terrorists, which frightened me even more.

Smoke leaned in and whispered. "Bruh, you scared?"

"Like a mu'fucka," I whispered back, unashamed to express how I felt.

"Same," he said. "Shit looks real out here."

I wasn't scared, as in, shook. I was frightened that something at any given moment could happen like . . . a bomb could go off or a shooter lightin' up the place. The soldiers had me on edge because it was something we weren't used to in America. Maybe a few policemen and throw in some airport security, but this was next level. If something happened to Kim and I couldn't protect her, I would die. I watched how crazy Africa could get on TV, which was something I didn't think about before booking our flight.

Kim leaned on the other side of my shoulder and whispered, "You scared, baby?"

I didn't want to tell her the truth because I wanted to be strong for her, but she probably overheard me talking to Smoke. "A little, are you?"

24

She looked at me and smiled, "Nah."

What she said shocked me, and for some reason, I believed her. At least someone's mind was together.

We exited the airport, and you could immediately tell we were out of place. The way people dressed, cars, buildings, roads, even the pavement . . . everything was different, and it felt different. It kind of gave off the feeling of a poor hostile environment. "We need to get a cab."

"Yo," Smoke waved down a white taxi with yellow front and back fenders. It was a van large enough to carry all of us.

"Good shit," I muttered as the cab stopped.

We walked up to the van, and the taxi driver got out to help. He opened the back hatch and said, "Welcome to Tripoli. Where would you like to go?"

He had a solid African accent, as expected. The clothes he wore told me that he was a Muslim which wasn't a problem. I put my suitcase and Kim's in the back trunk.

"You speak English," Smoke asked, shocked.

"Sir," the taxi driver said, "I speak many different languages. We have to learn how to communicate with the travelers if you want to drive."

"Bet," Smoke said, "Where the hoes at?"

"Smoke," Kim nudged him on the shoulder.

"What," Smoke asked sarcastically. "I'm just playin' with him."

"I'm sorry," Kim apologized.

"No need to worry, ma'am," the driver smiled. "Tourists come here all the time and ask where they can find a lady to bump, bump." He signed by pumping his hips.

"See," Smoke smiled. "I'm tryna bump, bump. You feel me," he slapped hands with the driver.

"Get your crazy ass in the van," she told Smoke.

The taxi driver shut the back hatch and got inside the vehicle. "Where would you like to go?" He said after we all piled in the back of the vehicle.

Kim spoke up, "To a nice hotel."

"One away from the city," I added.

The driver gave me a worried look. "I don't think that's a good idea, sir. That would be very dangerous. I don't think it would be good for the lady."

"Are there rebels around the area?" I asked.

"Yes, sir," he answered.

"Are there any other areas that are unoccupied by rebels?" I showed him the map. "Like this place." I pointed to the location."

"Mizdah, Libya," he said. "A guerilla group, sir, and refugees, mostly children. I can take you to a nicer part of Libya instead. Very nice, and the women are fine for your friends."

"No, I want to go to Mizdah."

"If I take you there," he said. "It would cost you double."

"I'll give you four times the amount for your trouble," I saw a smile spread across his face. "And one more thing."

"Sir, ask me anything."

I looked into his eyes and said, "Where can I purchase a gun?"

6 – Abel

Abel followed Oyoo out of the tent and noticed a plane flying overhead. The aircraft was low enough for Abel to see a woman staring back at him. It took two seconds before he had to look away. The rays from the sun caused his eyes to sting. He rubbed them while thinking the woman looked familiar, a close resemblance to his mother. Suddenly, the plane was gone.

"Are you okay?" Gina asked worriedly with a hand on his shoulder.

"I'm fine," he told her. It could've been the heat getting to him, so he shook the thought of the woman from his mind. "I wish I had brought some sunglasses." Oyoo was a reasonable distance ahead when he whispered to Gina, "Make sure you keep a close eye on him. Now that he knows we're carrying the diamond, he might go for it."

Gina didn't say a word, just nodded, assuring Abel she understood his command.

Oyoo walked over to the plane. "Gentlemen," after acknowledging them, he got on board.

Snake and Bam looked at each other confused. Sweat poured from their faces, making it clear to everyone that the heat had defeated them. While Abel and Gina were inside the tent, they were working their asses off unloading the plane. What kept them level-headed was Britt sitting inside the aircraft while they worked, and the two men got a few peeks of her breasts through her tank top. Sweat soaked her shirt, and they could see her nipples through it. She didn't give them any attention and never noticed the two eyeing her.

"What's wrong with driving the jeep?" Abel caught Oyoo at the door of the plane. Another plane ride wasn't what he had in mind. If that was the case, Silva should have stayed in the air.

Oyoo turned around. "If we use the Jeep, it will take eight hours to get there, and I don't have that much time. When that Jeep is moving, they expect a shipment of weapons. Do you have weapons for them?"

Abel understood what Oyoo meant. The Jeep didn't belong to him. It belongs to the army, and they use it to lead their shipments. Oyoo works for the General, so he doesn't want to be seen by his men. It could be dangerous for him. Abel sucked his teeth. "Load the plane," He looked at Snake and Bam before getting back on the aircraft.

Oyoo sat in the passenger's seat next to Silva and gave him the coordinates to the next landing zone. He knew a spot they could land without getting shot down.

Abel listened carefully to what Oyoo and Silva were conversing about. The two men worked with Jar and were apparently still involved in smuggling activities for the General.

"Do you think he'll try to set us up?" Gina whispered in Abel's ear, pretending just to kiss him. Although, she made sure Britt could see her tongue swirling around Abel's earlobe. When Gina saw the upset expression on Britt's face, she grinned, watching Britt cross her arms over her chest and look away.

"No, but he's doing a lot for nothing or an opportunity," Abel said, noting what Gina had done angered Britt. He didn't mind. Britt and Silva were lucky Oyoo decided to fly to the next destination. After they landed, the plan was to get rid of them and keep the plane for the trip back home. He couldn't trust Silva to stick around while they were working, and Britt had caused enough trouble. The two were safe for now.

Snake tossed the last of the ten bags onto the aircraft. His shirt looked like it had been sprayed with a water hose. He sat down next to Britt, took a deep breath, and looked at Abel. He wanted to say. *I'm your fucking best friend, so why are you working me so hard when you can get the others to do it? It's our dream to corrupt the government and cause havoc, not*

30

theirs. But he knew better. Abel had become someone else, someone terrifying. If somehow he gets through this alive, he plans to take his share and run.

Abel could tell by the look on Snake's face there was a problem. "Are you okay, my friend?"

Friend, Snake thought. *It doesn't seem like I'm your friend.* "I'm fine," he lied. "It's just the heat working me over."

"Good," Abel smiled. "I appreciate your help."

Bam shut the door, being the last to board the plane. He turned around and saw that every seat had been taken. "Come on," he sighed. After working as hard as he worked and come to find out all of the seats were gone pissed him off. He felt as if he was being treated the worst out of the bunch. "Where am I gonna sit?"

Gina spoke up, "On the floor where you belong, mutt."

Bam didn't want to smack Gina in the mouth for disrespecting him. He wanted to bust her in the face with a closed fist. "Ruff, ruff," he approached the situation differently. It was his way of saying, this dog bites. The sinister expression on his face was a dead giveaway. He wanted her to know he'd plan to murder her when this was all over. Bam didn't care what Abel thought at this point.

Nobody said a word for the next four and a half hours, partly because Gina fell asleep on Abel's shoulder.

31

Snake kept his attention on Britt. He wanted to say something to her but couldn't build enough confidence to speak.

Bam mean mugged Gina for two hours before closing his eyes, he appeared to be asleep, but he was actually thinking of different ways to kill her.

When Britt saw Gina asleep, she made it her business to lure Abel's eyes to her. She did everything in the book to gain his attention by tempting him secretly using seductive gestures.

Abel stayed completely aware of everything that went on. He pretended not to notice Britt, but she was too alluring for any man. Lucky for him, Gina was asleep. Silva and Oyoo had a few words between them. It was a short conversation about old times before Silva took it upon himself to sing aloud Bob Marly classics. Abel didn't mind the music, and surprisingly, Silva wasn't a bad singer.

"Over there," Oyoo pointed at the landing zone.

Abel adjusted Gina so he could look out of the window. They were flying outside of Tripoli, Libya. The landscape changed after passing over the desert, and so did the temperature to a small degree. He could see all the beautiful features of the city. They flew over a forest that divided part of the city from the ocean. As the plane lowered, he thought Silva was on a suicide mission. They were so close to the trees the wheels of the aircraft could touch them. A few seconds later, the

Mediterranean Sea came into view. It was a sight to see, and he woke up Gina so she could witness it from the air.

"It's beautiful," she awed at the view.

As they passed over the forest, Abel saw a dirt strip of land where the plane could land. It took Silva two minutes before he got the plane down on the surface. It wasn't the smoothest landing zone, but it worked.

Oyoo stood and turned toward everyone. He said with open arms, when all eyes were on him, "Welcome to North, Libya."

Abel stood, "Where is the doctor you speak of?"

"Not far," Oyoo assured him. "Just beyond the trees."

"In the forest?" Snake asked skeptically.

"No, in the city," he answered. "She's a doctor for people like us."

"What do you mean by that?" Snake questioned.

"The kind of doctor who doesn't keep records of who or what you are." Oyoo smiled and got off the plane. He was unaware that Snake and Bam knew nothing of Abel's condition.

"Okay," Snake looked at Abel. "Why are we here for a doctor?"

"To make sure we don't get sick," Gina lied for Abel. "Come on." She strapped her backpack around her shoulders.

"We're taking the luggage," Bam asked. "Through the forest, that's insane."

"No," Abel told him. "We'll set up camp offshore. We'll need a place to stay for the night before beginning our mission. Gina will come with me and Oyoo while you two set up the campsite." Abel grabbed his bag and got off the plane. He found a location hidden from view just beyond the trees. "This is where we'll rest until morning." He looked at Silva and Britt. "Don't go anywhere until I return. Once I'm back, you paid your debt."

"Yah, mon," Silva replied. That's exactly what he wanted to hear.

Britt didn't mind staying behind. The more time she got with Abel played in her favor. She wasn't planning to leave Africa with Silva anyway.

Abel walked up to Snake and put a hand on his shoulder. "I need you to keep an eye on them."

Snake nodded, "Of course."

"Can you get the radios to work while I'm gone?" Abel asked.

"Sure," Snake dropped his bag on the ground and opened it. "Take this with you."

"What is it?" Abel grabbed the device from Snake.

"It's a tracking mechanism," he told him. "I'll be able to find your signal if something happens to you. Wear it around your wrist like a watch. Click the button on the side, and the green compass will turn red on each watch and point to the threat's exact location. I made one for all of us and linked them together. Give this one to Gina."

It didn't surprise Abel how genius the idea Snake came up with was. During their time together in school, Abel saw Snake's bright ideas time and time again. His productions of unequivocal masterpieces were flawless. Abel signed in approval with a nod and strapped the device around his wrist. He gave the other to Gina before walking over to Oyoo. "Let's begin."

Oyoo smiled and led the way into the forest.

7 – Jordan

The gas indicator started flashing red. "We're out of fuel. I have to land, or we're gonna crash. Brace yourself." Adrian found a flat area of the land where he could land the plane. It was just outside a town.

Jordan sat down and strapped on his seat belt. He knew the landing would be rough and didn't want any undesired injuries. He looked at Rick and smiled. "You better sit down for this one, rook."

Rick felt the plane shaking and looked out of the window. "Fuck," he muttered, looking over the landscape. The path ahead was rocky, and several trees were along the way. It wasn't a straight path, and there was a slight possibility they could wreak. He sat down and strapped on his seatbelt.

Noti was strapped in the passenger's seat before Adrian decided on a safe enough landing zone. Her mind was elsewhere. It wasn't on the headquarters, receiving the money, or the sad look on Kane's face when she had left him. Her mind was on the devil in disguise, Abel. The son who murdered her husband.

Adrian held the controls tight as the wheels touched the rocky surface. His arms began to shake violently, and it took all of his strength to guide the plane to a safe stop. He let go of the wheel and exhaled, relieved they didn't crash. "That wasn't so bad."

"Bullshit," Jordan said. When Adrian looked back at him, Jordan pointed to the front window. "I guess you didn't see that fuckin' gigantic rock?"

Rick unstrapped his seat belt and looked in the direction of Jordan's eyes. He shook his head, grateful to still be alive. Adrian had stopped the aircraft in front of an enormous stone comparable in size to a minivan. The collision could have flipped the plane if hit at the right angle.

Jordan opened the side door and hopped out, not bothering to use the steps. He reached for a pair of sunglasses clipped to the neck of his shirt. "Better," he said as the dark aviator shades blocked the sun from his eyes. He looked toward the town and saw a few trees spread throughout the land, several large stones around the perimeter, homes, and buildings made of stone and clay. He thought the town could have been built in the early to the mid-19th century. The part of Africa they landed in was decades behind. He thought the chance of finding gas in the area was slim to none.

"It looks like we're gonna be stuck here for a while," Adrian said as he approached Jordan.

"Yep," Jordan said sarcastically.

Rick gently touched Noti on the shoulder, not trying to alarm her. "Are you alright, Mrs. Simmons?" she looked spaced out as if she wasn't aware they had stopped the plane.

Noti snapped back to reality. She had to focus on finding another way to the headquarters without Oyoo's help. She knew the location, but it's been over twenty years since she'd last returned to Africa and a year since her husband's death. Oyoo could've given up the location to the headquarters to another smuggler or the General. She didn't have enough intel to wander around the site, thinking it would be unoccupied. "Yes," she answered as if everything was okay.

Rick looked at her confused, "What did you mean by the devil has arrived?"

"It's none of your concern," she said.

"It is my concern because you're my concern," Rick had a serious look in his eyes. "And keeping us alive is my main priority. Jordan and Adrian are dangerous. You don't know who you're dealing with. You can't trust them."

"But I can trust you, Mr. Chase?" she asked evenly.

38

"Yes," he said. "You can trust me. I have to know what's going on to help. Help me, help you. It's the only way to keep us safe."

"I saw Abel," she turned away. "He's trying to find the headquarters. We have to get there before he arrives, or we're all going to die." She paused and sighed. "It's been long enough. We have to go before they suspect us of plotting against them." Noti didn't give him a chance to answer and never looked back before exiting the plane.

Rick sighed and viewed the others through the window. Jordan and Adrian were conversing when Noti approached them. He had a lot on his shoulders. The brothers were already enough to deal with, and now Abel was in play. He wondered if she actually saw him. She nearly passed out, and the expression on her face said she had. He didn't know what to make of the situation, and there was no way to inform the bureau of his whereabouts.

Jordan heard Rick get off the plane and turned to him. "Come with me to search the town. Adrian and Noti will stay behind and watch the plane." He saw the unhappy look on Rick's face. "What's with the face? It'll be like old times." He smiled and led the way toward a rocky pathway into town.

"That's what I'm afraid of," Rick muttered and walked past Noti and said. "Use the resources around you to make a weapon. It might come in handy if we don't make it back."

8 – General

The General and Abrafo walked out of his office into the corridor. The rebel leader had to not only die but suffer for raiding his camps. The General stopped in the main lobby where two of his men were waiting with hysterical looks on their faces. "Is there a problem?"

"General," both men saluted simultaneously and then acknowledged Abrafo. "Lieutenant."

The General recognized both soldiers. They worked in the air control division, monitoring Libya's border for unidentified airplanes trying to enter the country without consent.

"Continue," Abrafo told the taller of the two soldiers in their language.

"We spotted an aircraft just outside Tunisia," the soldier told them.

"The plane has entered our airspace?" the General asked evenly. He folded his hands behind his back. The facial expression he wore didn't show any signs of worry. A single plane wasn't anything to worry about unless it was the US military, a cargo plane, or attacking. Those were his only concerns. He didn't have enough resources to deal with every plane. There were more significant matters with the shortage of supplies and the rebels.

"Yes, General," he answered.

The other soldier signed with a nod when the General looked him in the eyes.

The soldier continued, "The plane crossed over the border, just passed the trees where it landed on the ocean side."

The General thought about the situation. He looked at Abrafo, whose mind wasn't clouded like his at the moment. "What do you suggest, lieutenant?"

Abrafo gave his opinion, "We should inspect the landing site. The traveler could be working with the rebels. We don't want to allow them to catch us not looking."

"Then it's settled," the General responded. He looked at the two soldiers and gave specific orders to carry out. "Go back to your posts, continue monitoring the airspace, and inform Lieutenant Abrafo immediately if the plane takes off. I'll send a four-man assault team to search the area and gather intel for you. Report back to me if there is any suspicious activity."

Both soldiers nodded, stood firm, and saluted the higher-ranking officers before departure.

The General watched the men leave the building before he spoke. "Do you think the rebels would send for help where we could easily spot them?"

"They're desperate enough to try anything, General," Abrafo said.

The General sighed, nodded, and continued to lead the way outside the building.

A fleet of vehicles waited for the General outside to escort him to the last campsite raided by the rebels. The lieutenant on-site reported the capture of a rebel during the raid. The General wanted Abrafo to interrogate the traitor personally. Several captured rebels chose death before giving up their leader. This time would be different. Abrafo specialized in interrogating terrorists. It was his first form of negotiating with smaller guerrilla units before rising through the ranks. This form of interrogation would last for days or even months. There wasn't a soldier alive who could resist the amount of suffering brought upon them. It was a configuration of slow and agonizing torture. In the shape of things to come, the soldiers would pray for the torment to end and eventually start to hallucinate Abrafo as the devil himself.

The General stopped beside the third Jeep in line behind two Humvees.

The soldier who opened the door for the General saluted both men.

The General saluted before entering the Jeep.

Abrafo spoke to the soldier. "An aircraft has landed outside of Tunisia. Possible help for the rebels. Take three men and search the area."

"I will address the issue immediately, lieutenant." The soldier saluted Abrafo.

"Air control will give you the location. Report any findings before engaging." Abrafo saluted the soldier and got into the Jeep with the General. He slightly nodded at the General, and the fleet of vehicles pulled away to where Abrafo would torment another traitor's soul.

9 – Kane

The taxi driver insisted we get a hotel room in Tripoli for the night. We found one off the coast overlooking the Mediterranean Sea. It would be safer, and he would come back in the morning to pick us up. He knew an independent gun trafficker toward Mizdah from who we could purchase guns. Until then, we would get settled and plan our day for tomorrow.

I paid the cab fare and said. "We'll see you tomorrow then?"

"Sir, I will be here in the morning." The man said. "I am now your driver."

"Sure you are," I said. "As long as we have American money."

The cab driver smiled. "My name is Aasir."

"Kane," I said. "See you tomorrow, Aasir. Don't spend that money bump, bumping all night. I need you here early."

"You have my word," he said.

I shook my head and stepped back from the van. I watched Aasir pull away in the cab. I picked up my bag and sighed.

Hopefully, what I said got to him, and he would be here bright and early. We needed protection. It was something we had to have while in Africa. Not because of the people or the environment. Tripoli was actually a nice place to stay. We needed weapons for what we were about to do. Every location won't be as welcoming as Tripoli. Depending on how far south of Libya we plan to go, those places will be hostile. Who knew where we would end up and the kind of situation that would arise. Mizdah was one of the pinned locations on my father's map that stood out and wasn't listed in his notebook. I thought that was odd because the other locations were, which I figured out by steadying the map on the plane ride. There was a reason why my father didn't list it in his notebook, and I wanted to know why.

I stepped inside the hotel and spotted the others. Kim was speaking with a customer service representative at the front desk, booking a room for us. I would imagine. Smoke, Bear, and Big Bruce were standing behind her like some uneasy bodyguards in unfamiliar territory. The hotel lobby didn't look all that bad. From the outside, looking at the building, you would think this place was a dump, but the inside looked immaculate. Everything inside was modern and didn't have the same feel as the 1920s look of the outside structure. I was surprisingly impressed with how clean the place had been kept, and the people didn't dress like other Africans. Maybe it was a part of welcoming tourists into a comfortable vocational stay at their hotel, which I thought was a good marketing strategy.

I walked over to my crew and stood next to them while waiting for Kim to finish. "Yo, this place isn't that bad."

"Bruh, we need a room overlooking the beach." Smoke said. "I'm tryna see the hizzoes."

"My guy," I said and gave him a look. "Focus, you know we're not here for that."

"So, we came all the way here and can't jump on any broads?" Bear said.

"Come on, Bear," I sighed. "Not you too."

"I mean," Big Bruce spoke up. "I see your woman. You're good. But a nigga can't enjoy one night? It's African. What kind of friendship y'all niggas have?"

"I'm fuckin' with him on this one," Smoke said. "And you know how we been acting."

"Same," Bear said. "We're on vacation. I wanna get jiggy."

"I wanna get jiggy," I muttered right when Kim turned around.

"I got two rooms across from each other," Kim said. "One for you guys and one for us."

"You got two rooms," I asked. "For what? How are we supposed to protect one another?"

47

"Boy," Kim signed. "I don't see anybody worried about us. You see this place. People are enjoying themselves. Nobody knows why we're here unless they followed us from America."

"True," Smoke broke in.

I looked at Smoke for cosigning. The look in my eyes told him I didn't apricate it.

"Why are you looking at him like that," Kim asked.

"Yeah," Bear said. "Why are you looking at him like that?"

"Don't be funny, Bear," Kim got on him.

Big Bruce chuckled.

"Don't you start," Kim looked at Bruce.

This is how it's been since high school. Kim didn't play with any of us. No matter how big we were or how much stronger. Kim made it known she was the boss. She's my girl, Smoke's sister, and Bear and Bruce's mother. And we all listened to her. What else could we do? We got dirty in the streets, been shot at, shot, and fought with a hitman, and still, Kim was right there to put us in our places. She doesn't take shit from anybody, which is one of many reasons I love her.

"This is what we're gonna do," Kim said. "We're gonna relax and have some fun on the beach tonight. Have and few drinks and enjoy Africa for at least one night. Unless you want me to give back the other key, and we stay together in one room." She held up the room key. "Which means . . . I won't be able to wear

48

that skimpy lingerie you bought for me with the see-through holes."

"Hell, yeah," Smoke spoke up.

"What," Kim said.

"Not for that," Smoke said. "Gross, you're my sister. I was referring to the beach idea. I'm tryna see some breezies."

"That's what I thought," Kim said.

"The one with the see-through private parts," I said. "You brought that?"

"Yep," she looked at me seductively.

I snatched the room key and gave it to Smoke. "Y'all niggas can't stay with us."

10 – Abel

Abel and Gina followed Oyoo through the forest toward Zuwarah, Libya. After thirty minutes of walking, the older man was gaining speed. Oyoo didn't seem tired at all and outpaced them by ten yards. He would turn around and smile at them every now and then. Abel's initial thought of Oyoo was that the older man looked frail, and there was no way he could survive in this type of environment. It was hot and muggy, and for the most part, Africa provided all sorts of danger. And yet, Oyoo moved around as if the land were his and there was nothing that could harm him.

Gina watched Oyoo move about through the forest. It was something mischievous about the man that she couldn't quite put her finger on. Abel ordered her to watch Oyoo, but she felt like the wise man was keeping an eye on her. "Why do I feel like he's watching us from the back of his head."

Abel maintained a half step in front of Gina. He said from the side of his mouth. "Because he is."

"It's been thirty minutes, and he hasn't slowed down one bit." Gina began to feel her legs give out. She sat on the plane for hours without moving them, and now they were getting a workout. She wanted to take a break but knew Abel wouldn't allow it. They were on a mission, and the love of her life needed medical attention. If Abel wouldn't stop, neither would she. "The forest didn't look this deep from the air."

Abel knew Gina was tired. He could see it on her face. She was strong and would keep up until the end. Gina was built that way, and that's why he fell in love with her. He spotted buildings up ahead through the woods. "We're almost there. The city is just up ahead." Abel did something he usually wouldn't do. He reached down and grabbed Gina by the hand and held it.

Abel didn't have to say a word. Gina felt his love. This was one of those rare occasions where Abel would show compassion. They would make it together. When their fingers interlocked, she completely forgot about her legs being weak. Killing Bam no longer clouded her mind, and Britt was an afterthought. The moment was reserved for them. And when they returned the diamond to the General and found Jar's headquarters. It would be them when it's all said and done. She would make sure of it.

Oyoo was the first to make it out of the forest onto the soil of Zurwarah. It's been months since he saw the doctor. The last time he visited her was when he needed a refill of different medications to keep in stock. Living in Mali alone in the middle of nowhere didn't provide the best healthcare or hospital access. People in his position had to care for themselves. Since he would be visiting, it made sense to refill while in the area. He stopped to let Abel and Gina catch up before continuing ahead.

Abel stood next to Oyoo and looked out to the city. "How far from here?"

"Two blocks," Oyoo informed him.

"Sounds good to me," Gina spoke up.

Oyoo turned to the side and looked into Gina's eyes. His face formed a broken smile as if to say you spoke too soon.

"What is it," Gina knew by the expression on Oyoo's face something was wrong.

Abel still held Gina by the hand when he spoke. "Rebels."

Oyoo nodded and faced the city.

"Where are they," Gina scanned the city and didn't see a soul. If Oyoo and Abel knew they were in rebel territory, why couldn't she spot them? Were they hiding, waiting for travelers to pass through the city to rob?

"They're not hiding," Oyoo read her mind. "They're positioned throughout the city to protect the doctor."

52

"Why," Gina said.

"From the General," Oyoo told her.

"I thought you worked for the General," she said.

"I do," Oyoo said. "That doesn't mean I don't have friends."

"The rebels are at war with the army," Abel said. "Raiding the General's campsites for weapons and supplies to survive. They believe the land belongs to them, and their political views are not the same. This is how it's been for a long time. Gun smugglers, drug and human traffickers are everyday life. If they don't give the General a percentage—"

"They're dealt with," Gina finished Abel's last statement.

"Move carefully with your hands out," Oyoo told them and made his hands visible to the rebels. "Show them we're not a threat."

Abel released Gina and held his hands out to the side. "What are you doing for them to allow you to pass safely?" he followed behind Oyoo.

Gina held out her hands and stayed close to Abel as she continued to search for rebels.

"In exchange for medication, I let them know when smaller gun smugglers come into the country with shipments. I get to see the doctor and live a longer life." Oyoo slowly stepped into the street to cross to the next block. He knew there was a gunman in the next building overlooking them with an assault rifle. The gunman didn't have to reveal himself for Oyoo to know he was there. There was always a gunman watching the street for unexpected vehicles.

"Playing sides," Abel said as he stepped into the street. He spotted a rebel inside the building in front of them. The gunman was positioned in a tinted window no bigger than 27 inches on the top level. The rifle barrel was barely visible through a cut-out space in the glass. As he crossed the street, Abel kept his eyes ahead. If he were to look, it could mean his life. He didn't want to give the gunman any reason to panic. "Keep your eyes forward."

"Okay," Gina said. She obeyed Abel's warning. Someone had eyes on them, and she didn't bother to find out the gunman's location. She was perhaps the most intelligent woman in Africa. And a high IQ couldn't match a bullet from any gun. Today wasn't her day to die.

Oyoo stopped in front of a door twenty seconds after crossing the street. "Just beyond this door, you'll get the care you need."

This was a moment of truth. Abel had the diamond on him, and Oyoo knew it. He could be walking into a trap. A building full of rebels wouldn't end well for them. Oyoo didn't give a reason why he decided to help. Could it be that Oyoo wanted him to replace Jar so he wouldn't have to work for the General? Maybe Oyoo was helping because he was Jar's son? Or maybe Oyoo was feeding him to the rebels like he did with other small smugglers? Abel hoped a doctor was on the other side but prepared for the worst. "Lead the way."

11 – Kane

Kim opened the door to our room, and I followed through behind her. The room was astonishing and larger than a three-bedroom apartment. It was enough space to throw a party for fifty guests. I watched Kim from behind as I stepped past the threshold. Damn, I couldn't help to look at the magnificent shape of her body. The way she walked turned me on. I felt like a young boy eyeing his hot babysitter. That one-in-a-lifetime chick you couldn't bang because of your age difference. And somehow, you stole a kiss, and she didn't tell your parents. Then you'd tell your friends about it the next day and become a hero. As time passed, you'd get older, and so would she. You'd never forget her or the first time you kissed an older hot woman. In the back of your mind, you told yourself if you ever saw her again. Well, you know what I'm about to say.

I put my bags down and approached Kim from behind. She was looking out the window toward the Mediterranean Sea. My hands gripped her waist on both sides. I towered over her, so I'd lowered my head down to her neck. Kim's right hand traveled around to my crotch. She messaged it as I gently began to kiss her neck. Her ass closed the distance between us. It didn't take much from her to wake the sleeping giant. She turned around, and her lips connected with mine. What she said earlier about enjoying one night, she wasn't wrong about it. We're in Africa, and how many opportunities do you get to experience another country? Trouble seems to follow me everywhere I go since Abel murdered my father. I had to take advantage of this moment with the love of my life. I can't speak for every man but for the few with the woman of their dreams as I am. Cherish the time you have with her. You get one chance in life to find meaningful love, and the women you thought you loved were just hot babysitters.

Suddenly, there was a knock at the door, interrupting our moment. "Go away," I shouted and went in for another kiss. My hands gripped Kim's ass as I pulled her closer.

"Bruh," I heard Smoke on the other side of the door. "We're tryna hit the beach before it gets late. I wanna see what the women look like before dark."

I sighed, frustrated. "Smoke . . .," I wanted to get some from Kim. She got me in the mood, and I could care less if they were at the door.

57

"And Bear," I heard the big guy.

"Bruce too," he said.

"We're waiting, bruh," Smoke said. "Put your dick up and open the door."

"Baby," Kim kissed me and pulled back a bit. "Let's go to the beach. We can get nasty later."

"Ah, man," I sighed.

"I promise we'll do it all night," she said. "In the bedroom, the living room, in front of the fireplace, the kitchen, bathroom, shower, and the balcony. Any and everywhere, baby."

I gave her a fake smile, "That's what friends are for, right?" I reluctantly released her.

"All . . . night . . . long," Kim kissed me and then walked over to the door. "How did you guys unpack your things that fast?"

"We didn't," Smoke said, walking through the door. "I tossed my shit on the bed and dipped."

"Same," Bear said. "I found a spot by the door and left it there."

"What," Kim said, shocked. "And I guess you did the same?" she looked at Big Bruce.

"I wasn't about to be the only one left in the room," Bruce said. "I'm not tryna miss out on anything."

"It doesn't look like y'all unpacked either," Smoke said. "And you're tryna get on us."

58

"Kane and I were talking about the beach," Kim smiled. "And what to do while we're there."

"Sure," Smoke said. "I bet his dick and your vagina were the only ones making plans for the beach."

"Ha," Bear laughed. "Dat nigga stupid."

I saw a smile on Big Bruce's face as well. They already knew what was up with us. I had to get my emotions in check. My soldier went from rock hard to soft when they walked into the room. It was over. I wasn't getting any until tonight. Cockblock, I thought.

"And they didn't have much of a conversation. Did they," Kim put her hands on her waist and gave them a look. "Cockblockers."

"Ah hell nah," Smoke said. "I know you didn't go there."

"Damn, she read my mind," I said, looking at Smoke.

"Y'all blocking my shit," Smoke continued. "We're supposed to be at the beach by now, having fun with the honey dips, smoking weed, and drinking. Y'all have time to bump bump later."

"Bump, bump," Bear said. "You heard the man." He flopped down on the couch.

"A . . .," Bruce held his hands up when Kim looked at him to speak next. "I don't have anything to do with it. I followed them."

"You know what," Kim sighed. "I can't with y'all right now. Imma get ready. How bout y'all?" She pointed at their clothes. "Y'all didn't think to change?"

"Hell nah," I said, looking at them. They had on the same clothes as before. Nobody thought to change. My mind was on Kim, and I wouldn't have noticed if she didn't mention it.

"Imma swim in my draws," Smoke said and chuckled. "Rock out with my cock out."

"Boy," Kim said sarcastically. "No one wants to see your whitey tighties."

"Ha," Bear chuckled.

"That explains why he's mad all the time," I heard Bruce mutter.

"Bitch please," Smoke said.

"What," Kim popped Smoke in the back of his head.

"Not you, sis," Smoke cried. "I'm talking to that nigga." He pointed at Bruce.

"Go change," Kim said and walked over to my bags. She pulled out my swim trunks and tossed them to me. "And take him with you."

"Babe," I cried. "What I do?"

Kim walked into the room and shut the door behind her. I heard it lock so that I couldn't enter.

"Collateral," Smoke said. "You're one of us."

60

"Shut up," I said. "You're the reason we got in trouble." I looked at Bear and Bruce. "Y'all come on and get ready."

Bear and Bruce followed me across the hall when I heard Smoke say, "Now you're the one cockblocking."

12 – Jordan

Jordan led the way into town. He didn't expect to be in a place like this three years ago. He was the top agent at the bureau and on his way to becoming the Deputy Director. A few more wins under his belt, and the spot would have been his without question. His career took a drastic turn when he lost the trial of the year. The trial that would have added to his argument as the top guy at the department. A student murdered his teacher with a baseball bat. The crime scene was gruesome. The teacher's face was brutally beaten. How could a student bring themselves to the point of destruction? Jordan found the murder weapon under the teacher's desk. Rick was his partner at the time, just a punk rookie cop he took under his wing. Everything was perfect, and life had been great until the judge banged his mallet. Kane was proven not guilty. Jordan was made a fool of on live television. It was the day everything changed. It wasn't losing the trial that ruined him. It was the ride back to the jail, watching Kane in the backseat of his police cruiser. That was the day Kane decided to enter his life. Not Jordan's life, but The Planner's. Kane exposed him for who he truly was, a monster.

Rick followed close behind Jordan. He wouldn't have predicted he'd be in this situation. *Backup,* he thought. *I should've called for backup.* It was a mistake to pursue Jordan without informing the Chief. Someone would surely know he was missing by now. It's been days since he'd been to work. It would've been different if he had a new partner after discovering Jordan's involvement with the diamond theft. The Chief sent an officer to his apartment after not showing up for work. That had to be the case. He was a missing federal agent. There was no sign of him at home or work, and his vehicle was vacated. The incident at the police impound set off an alarm. The shootout and the plane fleeing the scene. They knew it was him, right? Even if they did know it was him, they wouldn't know he'd be in Africa. They would never find him. Jordan and his wicked brother would kill him in the end. That would be his fate if he couldn't figure out how to take out Jordan while they were alone.

Jordan noticed Rick trailing behind, creating distance between them. He stopped and looked back at Rick. "Keep up. I don't want to think you're trying to escape."

Rick stopped and eyed Jordan. He couldn't see Jordan's eyes through the dark aviator shades. "Or what?" This was his chance. *You and me,* he thought. *Let's do it.*

"Or what," Jordan mocked with a smirk on his face. He didn't have to ask what Rick was thinking. What else would a cop have on his mind in this situation? At some point, Rick would try him while they were alone. Jordan knew all too well what a cop would do. He was one, in fact, the very best. There was something Rick didn't have enough of, and that was the experience.

Rick didn't say a word. He just kept his eyes on Jordan.

"You wanna hit me, tough guy," Jordan closed the space between them. It was hot out, and a trickle of sweat rolled down the side of Rick's face. Jordan knew that Rick was nervous about making a move on him, but he wasn't about to let Rick catch him slipping. If Rick wanted a piece of him, he'd get it. "Come on. Hit me."

Rick stood firm, eyeing Jordan as they stood nose to nose. They were standing in the middle of a deserted town in Africa. What better place to have a faceoff between former partners? Adrian wasn't around to help if Rick got the upper hand, but what if Rick couldn't take him? Then what? *What if I can't take him,* he thought. *He'll move than likely kill me, and no one would ever find my body. That wouldn't be good. Oh well, Rick. Be a man.* Rick had his fists balled tightly. He was ready to make a move but couldn't bring himself to swing on Jordan. In his mind, he kept thinking about what Jordan would do to him if he lost the fight.

Jordan's eyes traveled down to Rick's hands. *Yeah,* he thought. *He wants a piece.* Jordan took off his shades and clipped them on his shirt. He sucked his teeth while still in Rick's personal space. He stuck out his chin and pointed to it. "I'll give you a free shot."

What, Rick thought. *A free shot.* Rick couldn't believe what Jordan was doing. There was no way he could lose after a free lick, a lick that had to be a good one, powerful enough to knock him out. Rick's hands were no longer balled. They were shaking. At least he thought they were shaking. He was scared, and Jordan knew it. *Come on, Rick, be a man.* He sighed and took a chance. This would be the only opportunity he'd get for himself and Noti. He stepped back for better balance and threw a punch straight at Jordan's open chin. Halfway through the punch, he gained some confidence. Jordan hadn't moved. He was crazy enough to let Rick get a free one. Suddenly, not even an inch from Jordan's jawline. The blow Rick thought would be a knockout turned into an air shot. Rick's momentum carried him forward without control. *Dammnit,* he thought.

Jordan swiftly stepped to the side and let Rick take a swing at the air. Rick couldn't control his balance, and Jordan stuck out his foot. Jordan smiled as he watched Rick fall to the ground uncontrollably. A cloud of dust rose from under Rick like the aftereffects of an explosion. Jordan thought it was hilarious watching Rick sprawled out on his stomach. "Look at you." Jordan kicked dust in Rick's face. "You're not even worth my time."

The dust entering Rick's nose made him cough hard. *Dammit,* he thought. It was a mistake to think he could trust Jordan. A free shot. That was a load of bullshit. Jordan made him look like a foul. Rick slowly got up from the ground. Dirt covered his clothes, and he dusted himself off, thinking about his mistake. Although it didn't go in his favor, Jordan didn't attack him. A face full of dirt was worth the risk, better than being left for dead. "I have to give it to you. You're a man of your word."

"And you're still a dumb rookie co—" Rick unexpectedly rushed Jordan, spearing him to the ground. *What the fuck,* he thought. His guard was up while lying on his back, blocking Rick from punching his face.

"You sonovabitch," Rick growled, trying to land a shot on Jordan's face. His punches weren't getting through Jordan's guard, so he threw a few blows to his gut. While he had the upper hand, he had to figure out what to do next. Jordan would eventually overpower him. Rick wasn't as strong as his former partner. There was something he couldn't do, let Jordan reach for his gun.

Jordan laughed as he blocked every single shot Rick threw at his face. It was exciting to him. These were the moments he lived for, the moments The Planner enjoyed being a part of. There was nothing better than being in a tough situation. It's been too long since he'd satisfied his hunger for danger. "Come on, Rocky. You can hit harder than that."

What the hell is wrong with him, Rick thought. Jordan's twisted mind had him laughing on his back while being punched. Rick couldn't think straight. Jordan enjoyed a beating, and it screwed with Rick's thinking process. To make matters worse, he felt fatigued, and Jordan was making jokes. If he stopped punching, Jordan would win. Rick wouldn't have any strength left to defend himself. There was only one thing left that came to mind. Get Jordan's gun. Two places it could be, he thought, back or side waistband. Rick swiftly reached for Jordan's waistband while simultaneously taking a shot to the face. He knew it would happen, but it was worth it. He fell off to the side. His nose felt broken as he groaned in pain.

Jordan took the open opportunity to hit Rick in the nose. He figured Rick would eventually tire out from missing punches. As

Rick fell off to the side, he hopped on his feet. He laughed wickedly as he kicked Rick in the side. "On your stomach again, rook." He kicked Rick a second time as he tried to crawl away. "Where are you going? We're in the middle of nowhere in a deserted town." Another kicked. "Without any fucking," another kick. "Gas." Jordan stood there and watched Rick for a moment. "It's time to end this." He reached for his gun, and it wasn't there. "What the—"

"Look at you," Rick was lying on his back with Jordan's gun pointed at him. He cautiously got back on his feet while keeping the weapon on Jordan. "And you're supposed to be the vet."

Jordan smiled devilishly at the barrel of his gun. *Sonovabitch,* he thought. Rick pulled a move on him. He had to admit that he didn't see it coming. Jordan's eyes shot beyond Rick. Something else caught his attention. "This is your hero moment."

Kill him, Rick. The smile on Jordan's face kept Rick from pulling the trigger. There was something peculiar about it. As if Rick had missed something. *What are you not telling me,* he thought. Deep down, he wanted to know what Jordan was thinking before ending his life. "Wipe that silly smile off your face. You're about to die."

"I think we both are," Jordan signed with his index finger, letting Rick know there was something he hadn't noticed. Then, he held up his hands.

"You think I will fall for another one of your tricks," Rick said. When they entered the town, it was empty. No one was around. There weren't any signs of life. Jordan didn't expect Rick to reach for his gun. Now that he had it, Jordan was just trying to figure a way out of the predicament. *Stop wasting time, Rick, and kill him.* "It's over." Suddenly, Rick was struck in the back of the head. He fell to the ground and dropped the gun. He heard Jordan laughing in the background. *Adrian,* he thought while turning over on his back. His eyes grew after noticing who'd hit him. A group of rebels with assault weapons surrounded them. One stood over him with a gun aimed at his forehead. His eyes wandered over to Jordan. The rebels had him at gunpoint as well. The one time he should've listened to Jordan, that was it.

One of the rebels tied Jordan's hands behind his back. The situation was more exciting now than before. They were in hostile territory. There wasn't a doubt thought in his mind. He wouldn't have thought he'd be in a more difficult situation than infiltrating the notorious TMF. The mafia was one thing, but African rebels were on a larger scale. A single cop wouldn't be able to escape a situation like this one. There was only one person who could, The Planner. As the rebels walked Jordan past Rick, he said. "You blew your hero moment, rook."

13 – Kane

I finished dressing, and so did the rest of my crew. I put on a wife-beater and swim trunks with images of different color goldfish. Big Bruce put on solid blue trunks and a wife beater. Bear looked almost identical to Bruce. The only difference was his trunks were solid white. Smoke was another story. This guy wanted people to know he smoked.

"My guy," I looked at Smoke.

"What," Smoke held his hands out and made a funny face at me.

"Weed trunks," I said, looking him over. Smoke had on light green trunks with a giant marijuana symbol on the front and back.

"And, my guy," he picked up a bottle of sunscreen. "Look at what you're wearing."

"What about it," I asked.

"Goldfish, nigga," he said. "As big as you are. You're wearing kid trunks."

"These aren't kid trunks," I said, looking down at my shorts. Kim likes these. She picked them out for me before we left America. I didn't actually think we'd go to the beach.

"Shittin' me," he said.

"Bear," I said. "Does it look like I'm wearing kid trunks?"

"I mean," Bear didn't finish.

"Bruce," I said. "What they look like?"

Bruce didn't say anything. He just held out his arms and sighed sarcastically.

"Man . . . fuck y'all," I said.

They started laughing.

"Come on," I walked to the door. "Let's go before Kim get on our heads."

"You're head," Smoke said. "That's your girl."

"You want me to tell her what you said," I asked.

Smoke thought about it for a moment. "Hell nah."

"Aight then," I opened the door. "Let's ride." I was the first to walk outta the hotel room. I stepped across the hall to the room I was staying in with Kim. I'd left the room key inside with her, so there was no way for us to enter. Just before I was about to knock, the door opened.

Kim stepped out into the hallway. "Look at you guys." She said with a smile.

Damn, even though I knew what Kim looked like without clothes. Her body was still magnificent. I couldn't take my eyes off her. She had on a Jamaican color two-piece swimsuit with green sandals with a gold flower over the top. She'd wrapped her dreads in a bun with one loose in the front, hanging off to the side. I could barely see her eyes through the tinted pair of aviator shades she wore. Her body was glistening from the scented oil she put on. I could smell the aroma coming off her body, filling the air. I was staring at her, stunned, when I heard.

"Snap outta it, playboy," Smoke snapped his fingers in front of my face. "You can hit that later."

I shook my head as if I was stuck in a trance and just found my way out. I looked at my crew, and they were looking back at me with raised eyebrows. All three of them had puzzled looks on their faces as though something was wrong with me.

"You're in love, bruh," Bear said. "I need to experience that."

"You're not the guy I was locked up with," Big Bruce added.

"Take it easy on my man," Kim wrapped her arms around my neck. "You guys are just jealous." She kissed me on the lips.

"Aw . . . shit," Smoke said. "Let's get outta here. I can't stand to watch them get all lovely dovey."

"Right," Bear said and followed Smoke down the hallway.

73

"Right behind you, bruh," Big Bruce followed in their footsteps.

Kim's arms were still wrapped around my neck, and I didn't want her to let go. I could've stood there all day with her. The woman who stunned me every time I saw her. My first and only love of my life. The woman I'd kill for without a doubt in my mind. She meant everything to me.

"Let's get out of here before they get lost," she said.

I kissed her one more time and said, "Okay."

Kim and I caught up with the crew just before the elevator opened. We got on and headed down to the main floor of the hotel. We walked through the lobby, and I felt like everyone in the building was staring at Kim. Even the women. She was the center of attention, and I wanted to wrap a towel around her to cover her ass. I couldn't do it, though. What type of man would I be if I easily get offended when someone is staring at my woman? She's with me, and that's what matters most.

We left the hotel and walked for about five minutes before touching the sand of the Mediterranean Sea. I made a mistake by wearing Jordan's to the beach. Everyone had on shoes except for Kim. She was the only one who could walk across the beach without sand filling her shoes. I'd quickly took them off, tied the strings together, and tossed them around my neck. As expected, my crew did the same.

When Kim got a bit ahead of us, Smoke said, "Man, the hoes are out tonight."

"No kiddin'," Bruce said, scanning the women in the area.

"If I don't get any tonight," Bear said. "It ain't happenin'."

"Then it ain't happenin'," Smoke said. "Cause you'll be sleep, nigga."

I chuckled, and so did Bruce.

"You want me to kick your ass," Bear dropped his things.

"Wassup," Smoke dropped his stuff as well.

Smoke and Bear began to play fight like friends do when one tests the other. Smoke was much faster, and he ran circles around Bear, slapping his head several times before the big man could react.

"He's gettin' in your ass, dawg," Big Bruce said. "Where's that energy you had at the house?"

I chuckled at that one, but I knew Smoke would only have the advantage for a brief moment. And that moment was up.

"Oh shit," Smoke said as Bear caught his arm and reeled him closer.

"Ut oh," I muttered. "It's over."

Bear grabbed Smoke and bodyslammed him in the sand. They both were laughing the entire fight. Smoke tried his best to get up, but Bear held him down with one hand. That's how much stronger he was than Smoke.

"Say you're sorry," Bear joked.

"Never, nigga," Smoke laughed out while struggling to move. "I'm bout to kick your ass when I get up."

"Nigga," Bruce said. "You ain't gettin' up."

I chuckled, "Hell nah."

"Hey," everyone stopped and looked over at Kim. She was standing with her hands on her hips, which showed that we were in trouble. "Come on before I kick your butts. I need help setting up the umbrella."

Bear let Smoke up from the ground. Sand had gotten all over Smoke, and he brushed it off.

As they walked over to us, Smoke said to Bear. "You're lucky. I was gettin' in your ass."

"Both of y'all would've lost to me," I joked.

"Nigga," Smoke said. "Go set that umbrella up before Kim whips your ass."

I swiftly grabbed Smoke and slammed him into the sand before Kim could notice. "Dick runs the show. Don't forget it."

14 – The General

The Jeep the General rode in pulled up to the campsite last raided by the rebels. A soldier on-site managed to capture one of the traitors. Abrafo would interrogate the traitor and get information on their leader's next move. The rebels decided to move against the General. They felt there was no need to work with the army or pay them for smuggling guns, drugs, or women in and out of the country. There was a profit to be made, and the dealings would end if it weren't paid to the army. Under the command of the General, the rebels would be free to move, but they desired otherwise. The rebels deployed other tactics to evade the army and started fighting back when their men were hung for being deceitful. The General had to set an example for dioloyol compatriots. The rebels were a strong guerilla unit, and the General had to break them by using brute force.

The Jeep shut off, and the men exited the vehicle. The General stood next to Abrafo and scanned the area. The scene looked like there was a small war. The campsite was a post to transport military supplies for the army. The rebels infiltrated the site by disguising themselves as smugglers who wanted to deal with the General. After his men discovered them, a war broke out. The General could see dirt patches where bullets ricocheted off the ground. Most of the tents had bullet holes, and he noticed some had caught fire. There was smoke still fuming off them, filling the air with an awful burnt small. The bodies stacked on top of each other in a pile in the camp center made it evident that rebels had made contact.

The soldiers in the Humvees stood by the vehicles while the General and Abrafo walked over to the bodies. A soldier stood next to the pile, waiting to burn the bodies. The soldier saluted as they approached, and they saluted him.

The General was the first to speak. "How many men died today?"

"Twelve, General," the soldier answered.

"How were they killed," the General looked at the bodies. He was short of men and now had to replace the lost soldiers. The campsite was one of his top priorities.

"The rebels intercepted one of our trunks," the soldier said. "They used one of our men to infiltrate the camp. Two guards watching the gate were shot in the head upon arrival. Five soldiers hurried over, and the truck exploded, killing them all.

The rebels were not in the truck. At least ten rebels got inside the camp before responding to the threat. They cut through the fence around the perimeter. Another vehicle arrived with an assault team. They took supplies and set fire to the tents. I shot one in the leg before he could escape with the others."

The General sighed and nodded. The rebels were getting smarter with their tactics. The General didn't expect them to take down one of his highly guarded campsites. "Where is the traitor?"

"We have him in the tent," the soldier pointed to the location. "There."

"Well done, soldier," the General informed him. "Burn the bodies and get word to their families." He saluted the soldier and headed for the tent, holding the traitor.

"Over thirty men position at the camp," the General started. "And the rebels escaped with our supplies with ten men. What are we training to be? How did we only capture one man and kill none?"

Abrafo knew what the General was implying. This was on him. He was the leader of the army and the man who trained them. The General didn't bother to look at him while he spoke. They were friends, but he would never put it past the General to have him murdered. They were supposed to be iron welled under his command. Abrafo would take the soldiers and turn them into warriors. A small bunch of rebels should not be able to infiltrate their camp with fewer men. There was nothing Abrafo could say, and the only way to fix it was to get the information from the traitor.

The General was the first to step inside the tent. There were two soldiers inside, waiting for them to arrive. The soldiers stood firm with guns on their sides and saluted their superiors. The General returned the gesture before walking over and standing in front of the traitor. It disgusted him to lay eyes on the rebel. The traitor wore their uniform, disguising himself as one of them. The General's eyes trailed down to the leg where the traitor had been shot. Dirt covered his face and clothes, and he smelt of musk. The traitor looked exhausted as if he'd been at war for days without food or water. Under the dirt on his face, the General could see that his eyes had swelled from getting beaten. The traitor held his head downward and didn't have the strength to acknowledge the General's presence. The General stepped closer and raised the rebel's head with a finger under his chin. "You will tell me what I want to know."

The rebel managed a desperate attempt to smile and spit at the General.

Abrafo backhanded the traitor hard enough that the chair fell back with him in it. Then he removed a handkerchief from his pocket and wiped the General's jacket.

"Strip him of our uniform," the General ordered. "He isn't worthy of it. Then burn his feet because he doesn't deserve to stand as a man on African soil."

The two soldiers lifted the traitor and began to remove his uniform. He was left naked and tied to the chair when they finished. Before Abrafo was able to start torturing the rebel, his phone rang.

"Lieutenant," the soldier over the phone spoke. "We are at the site where the plane landed."

"Continue, soldier," Abrafo said.

"There are four foreigners," the soldier said, watching their movement by the plane. "Three men and a woman. I don't see any military supplies. They could be here to pick up weapons from the rebels. They are setting up camp by the beach."

"I want to know why they're here," Abrafo said. "Move in and use force if necessary."

"Yes, lieutenant," the soldier replied. "I will report after contact."

Abrafo ended the call and relayed the information to the General. After speaking with him, it was time to work. He turned his attention back on the traitor. He removed a lighter from his pocket—the same golden lighter decorated with the flag of Libya on each side he uses daily to smoke cigars. He flicked open the lighter with his thumb, making a hollow sound as if hitting the

81

side of a cup. "Hold his feet," he ordered the soldiers and when they got the rebel in position after a brief struggle. Abrafo crouched down to get closer and lit the lighter. The traitor began to scream and struggle with the soldiers, trying to kick his feet away. The flame seemed only to brighten Abrafo's face while in front of him, illuminating his dark eyes. This terrified the rebel, and Abrafo was yet to begin.

The General smirked, listening to the frightened man beyond the dirty face. His cries made the General feel in control and powerful. To break a man down and have him cry for help was a pleasure. It was the difference between snakes and how they crush prey before a kill. To crush every bone in the body while you live through it defines the predator. You had to look into his eyes while excruciating pain destroyed your body. "Abrafo," the General waited for their eyes to meet. "Take your time. I want to enjoy his cries."

15 – Kane

After setting up the umbrella, Kim and I settled under it while the boys were out chasing women. We didn't prepare for a weekend vacation. The only thing we had to lay on were the towels Kim brought in her bag. It was cool, and we enjoyed the moment we had together. I needed to take my mind off everything that had happened over the past few months. The scenery was incredible, and I had my girl by my side. I couldn't have asked for more.

"This is nice and peaceful for a change," Kim said while laying on her back and looking over at me. She sighed and smiled.

"It is," I said. "I'm happy to share this moment with you." I looked back at her. She had taken off her glasses so I could see her beautiful eyes.

She kissed me on the lips. "Do you think we'll find your mother?"

"If she's here," I said. "We'll find her." There was nothing between us except for sand and a few tiny seashells. I could hear the waves from the ocean rise on the shoreline and then fade away. I'd never experienced anything like this before now. This was technically my first vacation day with friends. As if we were taking a vacation with friends in our senior year to another country. That one time you were without your parents, far off where they couldn't tell you what to do.

"I still can't believe she decided to leave with The Planner," she said and looked off to the side. "I wonder if he's forcing her?"

I began to think about my mother. The Planner could be forcing her to bring him to my father's headquarters. When I spoke to her before she got on the plane, she didn't mention anything. It seemed like she wanted to go with them as if it was something she needed to do. No matter the reason she went with them. I need to find her. The Planner was the person who put me through hell, and now he has my mother. He kidnapped her from the hospital, so I know there's something more. He needs her for something, and it's not to get at me. Abel has the diamond. If the Planner wanted it from me, we could've negotiated at the impound. My mother and Kim are the most important people in my life, and I would go to the end of the earth for them.

"I know my mother wouldn't willingly go with him," I said. "At the same time, she's strong enough to take care of herself. The way she looked into my eyes at the impound. I could tell she'd changed. She'll be okay. But, what I want to know is . . . why do you look so sexy?" I changed the subject. I love my mother, and I plan to find her. At this very moment, it was our time—me and Kim. I wanted her mind to be free from The Planner, Abel, and anything other than being happy. My time belonged to her.

She smiled at me and pulled on my hair—the thing she always does to show her affection for me. "I love you, Kane Simmons," she said passionately.

"I always and will forever love you," I told her.

She kissed my nose and said. "Let's go for a swim?"

"Okay," we got up, and I followed her into the water. "Ah, cold."

"You big baby," she said and splashed water in my face.

"That's how you wanna play," I splashed water back at her. The water felt good once I managed to get my body wet. Kim was a better swimmer than me. Her body was built for it. I wouldn't say I liked the water as much as her, but it was nice.

We spent about thirty minutes playing in the ocean before it began to get dark. I spotted the boys chatting with a group of females in a gazebo. It looked like they were serving drinks as well. I pointed over for Kim to see. "You wanna grab a drink, gorgeous?"

"Sure, handsome," she said.

As we began to walk over, a kid ran up to me. "Hey, mister. I like the fishies on your shorts." He chuckled and hurried off to his mother.

Kim giggled. "That kid has good taste."

Fuckin' kid shorts, I thought. I'm glad Smoke wasn't around to hear him. He would've had a good laugh. I wanted to bodyslam that kid like I did Smoke earlier. I noticed Kim looking at me funny. "What," I said. She could tell when my mind summoned bad intentions.

"You know what," she said, grabbing my hand and pulling me towards the pavilion.

"I wouldn't hurt a kid," I said playfully. "I just wanna show him who's boss."

We approached Smoke and the others. The DJ was playing Afrobeat music. It was a chill vibe, and weed smoke clouded the area. My crew and three other women were passing two blunts between them. Everyone was getting high and drunk. I looked around the pavilion and noticed they weren't the only ones having a good time, so I guess it was cool.

"I smell Kush," Kim spoke as she pulled up a chair.

"You know it, sis," Smoke passed the blunt to Kim, and she took a hit.

I looked at Bear. "You smoke, big guy?" I didn't know Bear got down like that. I'd only smoked with Kim and Smoke.

"Doesn't everyone," Bear responded coolly. His eyes were red and low.

"Okay, and you too, Bruce," I said.

"This ain't new to me," he replied.

Damn, I thought. Everyone's eyes were red from being high. They were laughing at Smoke and Bear talking about their fight.

Smoke began to fabricate the story as I pulled up next to Kim. Smoke stood and said. "Then I slammed his big ass." He signed with his arms as if he was bodyslamming Bear to the ground.

"Here, baby," Kim passed the blunt to me.

"Aw . . . hell nah," Bear said. "This nigga lying."

The women chuckled at Smoke as he told his side of what happened.

I hit the blunt and just listened as if I didn't see what actually went down. Kim and I ordered more drinks. By the time I got to the third one, I was fucked up. Man, I could feel myself losing control. I was at the point where I needed to get back to the room before I couldn't walk straight. I looked over at Kim, and she didn't look as bad. I knew she was at least tipsy. The drinks

87

tasted like the bartender only poured alcohol in them. I guess the way everyone would like them made if you're trying to party.

"This nigga lit," Smoke said, puffing on the blunt.

"My guy does look fucked up," Bear said. "You good, bruh? Do you want me to carry you home?"

Everyone laughed.

"Funny," I said.

The girl next to Bear spoke up. "You don't want to carry me home?"

"Fo' sho," Bear said.

The girl smiled and said in an African accent. "American men are funny and strong." Her tiny hand grabbed Bear's bicep and squeezed. "Your arm feels like a rock."

"That ain't the only thing that feels like a rock," Bear looked at her.

She smiled at Bear. I chuckled, thinking my boy had game. She didn't look bad, and neither did the other two women. They were cute African women with nice bodies. Probably, looking for American men to take home for the night. They didn't look much older than us. Two of them had close hair cuts while the third sported longer hair. She was the one next to Smoke and looked better than her friends. I knew it would go down tonight in both rooms by the look on everyone's faces.

Kim whispered in my ear, "I'm ready for you."

Oh shit, I thought. I knew what that meant. "A'ight, fellas. We're outta here. You know the way back." I stood, and so did Kim.

Smoke gave me some dap. "A'ight, my guy. See you in the morning."

I dapped Bear and Bruce. "In the morning."

"See you guys later, and nice meeting you ladies," Kim smiled and waved goodbye.

We got back to the hotel room quicker than it took to get to the beach. Kim was all over me as I backed into the bedroom. Our clothes led from the front door to the bed, which wasn't much. I had her in my arms with her legs wrapped around my waist.

"Uh, uh, uh," Kim moaned as I thrust inside her.

I didn't take her to the bed. I held her up in the air for a while, pleasuring her. I was giving her the business, working her over as she kissed the sides of my neck and chest. She grinded her pelvis against mine, trying to force my manhood deeper. I felt her get wetter than the Mediterranean Sea. It felt like heaven inside Kim. I put her down and bent her over the bed doggystyle. She tooted her ass in the air, and I held onto her hips. I would imagine you could hear the clapping sound down the hallway. It was that loud. I smacked her ass the way she liked it.

"Oh, Kane," she moaned, throwing her ass back.

"Um," I pushed deeper and held it there for a moment. Kim's legs began to shake uncontrollably, and I felt a different kind of moisture.

"I'm cumming, baby," she cried. "Don't stop."

I wasn't ready to stop. I was a bit drunk and high. I could go for hours. When she finished cumming on my manhood, I flipped her over. I wiped myself off before going back inside. "Wrap them sexy legs around me, baby." I laid on top of her and pounded that pussy. I long stoked her for about twenty minutes, making her cum two more times.

"What the fuck are you doing to me," she moaned. "I fucking love you."

That's right, I thought. Because I'll fucking kill a nigga for you. I was deadly in love with Kim. She was all mine and would be my wife. I growled as I felt myself about to erupt. My manhood began to pulsate, and I knew she felt it.

"Don't pull out," she said while holding my ass and pulling me closer. "I want you to cum inside me, baby."

Every time we had sex, it would end with me cumming inside her. One day, Kim would tell me she was pregnant and make me the happiest man on earth. "Fuck," I came and broke down while still inside her. "Damn," I sighed. It got better and better each time.

Kim put her leg over my waist as we lay there naked. "I love you."

"I love you too," I kissed her forehead. This was the only place I wanted to be in the world. Next to my girl, sharing an intimate moment. I wanted to enjoy it while it lasted because, in the morning, I would be on the hunt for my mother and The Planner.

16 – Abel

The door opened, and a rebel soldier greeted them with an assault rifle. Abel was more massive than the soldier and could easily take him. The soldier kept his AK-47 on Abel because he was the largest. He had to tilt his weapon upward as he steadied the others. He'd seen Oyoo before, but Abel and Gina had him cautious. The soldier said something in Arabic that only Oyoo could understand.

Abel kept his eyes on the rebel. The soldier's voice was stern, and he had a dangerous look in his eyes. Abel knew the rebel would be hostile. It's customary with rebel soldiers in foreign countries. After spotting the soldier in the window, Abel figured this wouldn't be a walk in the park. They had to show they weren't a threat. He kept calm, wondering what the soldier said to Oyoo.

Gina's blood began to simmer. She was furious because the rebel was holding Abel at gunpoint. She had to get her emotions in check before the soldier noticed her anger. She eyed the soldier with contempt, and he turned the weapon on her.

"Turid almawt!" the soldier shouted at Gina.

Oyoo stepped in front of Gina and blocked the rebel's gun. He held his hands up, showing the soldier they had come in peace. The soldier had asked Gina if she wanted to die. It was a clear sign that the rebel was seconds away from shooting her. "Nahn nazur altabib."

"The doctor," the soldier spoke in broken English. His eyes flickered between them.

He can speak English, Abel thought. Oyoo had calmed the rebel by letting him know their reason for visiting. It hadn't been five minutes, and the soldier was ready to kill Gina. They would have a short life if she continued with an aggressive approach.

"Why do you want to see the doctor," the soldier asked, stepping back so he could keep clear of his weapon getting taken.

"We need medicine," Oyoo told the soldier. The only time the soldier questioned Oyoo in depth was on his first visit. Any other time, Oyoo would give information on smugglers before arriving. The doctor would inform the soldiers he would visit. On this occasion, Oyoo needed to speak to her in private. If he had communicated his reason for coming, the call could've gotten intercepted by the General.

"The doctor isn't expecting anyone," the soldier said. "They're smugglers. Why not inform us first? You want to take our medicine!" He held up his weapon, ready to shoot.

Oyoo made a mistake by not contacting the doctor. This was how it had to be if he wanted them to travel safely. The rebel was on edge, and there was only one way to calm him before he pulled the trigger. "This is the son of Jar."

The rebel's eyes grow wide as if in fear. "La aant takdhib!" the rebel stuck his weapon in Oyoo's face.

The soldier thought Oyoo was lying. His nose touched the tip of the gun. "An 'artakib hadha alkhata." He wanted to let the rebel know that he wouldn't make a mistake like that and reveal himself to danger.

"You," the rebel said in broken English. "Come here to die pretending to be someone you're not." He wanted to pull the trigger but couldn't without finding out the truth. If he killed the man before him, it could also mean his life.

Abel was confused for a brief moment, thinking about how the soldier reacted to Oyoo calling him the son of Jar. Mentioning Jar struck fear in the rebel's eyes. *Why would he be frightened of Jar,* he thought. There was something Oyoo hadn't told him, and it wasn't about the diamond. What did his father do to make even a hostile rebel fear killing him without being present? Was Jar that powerful to them?

"Speak," the rebel said sternly.

Gina wasn't angry anymore because her mind was distracted by the same question that Abel pondered. What was wrong with the rebel soldier, and why was he terrified of Jar?

"I am," Abel said evenly as he wasn't afraid to die. He waited on the rebel to respond but saw that he was hesitant. Not even a second later, Abel noticed a figure in the background in the shape of a woman. He took his eyes off the soldier to focus on the shadowy figure. He couldn't believe his eyes when the woman stepped into the light. "Mother," he muttered.

The woman was close enough to hear Abel's whisper of uncertainty. "No . . . I'm your aunt."

17 – Jordan

Jordan sat across from Rick. The rebels had put them in a small room built for prisoners. The room was in a barn-like shed across from a large building made of stone. The smell inside the room was horrific, and neither could tolerate the odor. They could see the remains of another prisoner on the ground. A giant rat crawled through the rib cage of the bones. The body of the prisoner was left for dead. There wasn't any telling how long the body had been inside the room without food, water, or sunlight. There was a tiny opening in the door they could see out of, no bigger than a pocket-size wallet. They had to come up with a plan or end up like their new roommate, which meant . . . they had to work together.

Jordan leaned back against the wall. He was tired of hearing Rick cry about their current situation. At some point, he would murder Rick for getting on his last nerve. At the very least, that's what The Planner wanted to do, but the cop side reminded him not just yet. He needed Rick to get out of this predicament, even if he used Rick as bait. That's what he'd do, survive or die like the dog in front of him. He didn't want a rat crawling through his body. What kind of ending what that be for a criminal mastermind? He had to leave The Planner on the sideline and be Jordan for now.

"I can't take it anymore," Rick backed away from the door. He was looking through the hole, trying to get a visual of the rebel's operation. He was doing what he normally does, being a detective. "It smells like shit, and I can hardly breathe." He began to cough and bent over with one hand on his knee and the other covering his mouth. "How can you just sit there as calm as you are? You wanna die here? Let's try to kick the door down or something?"

Jordan sighed. "Look at the guy on the ground. How many times do you think he tried to kick the door down?" It wasn't possible. The rebels were innovative by using a fire wooden door. It looked like a door created in the 1800 century that belonged in a castle.

Rick looked over at the body of bones. *Shit,* he thought. Jordan was right. They wouldn't get through the door that way. He searched deep in his mind for a solution but couldn't think of any bright ideas. "What do you suppose we do?"

"Don't know," Jordan said. "Maybe we should die." He smirked still with his head back as if he didn't care.

"As long as you die first," Rick said. "I'll be okay with it." He looked through the hole again, trying to figure out a way through the heavy door.

"So you can eat the flesh from my dead body," Jordan said. "I wouldn't give you the pleasure, Hannibal."

"You don't have a choice," Rick said. "I have more meat on my bones, so I'll survive longer than you, Chris Rock."

Jordan chuckled. "I have to admit that was a good one."

"The devil laughs," Rick said without looking and keeping his focus through the door hole. While his nose was at the door, it caught a different scent other than the smell inside their prison. "Do you smell gas?"

"What," Jordan said.

"I smell gas," Rick sniffed the air. "I'm sure of it. Right outside the room."

"Kerosene," Jordan questioned. "What you smell is piss and shit from a dead guy."

"Trust me," Rick said and backed away from the door. "See for yourself."

"So you can attack me from behind," Jordan said. "You think I'm a fuckin' idiot, rook?"

"I think you're a dumbass," Rick said. "If I wanted to kill you for some reason. I'd wait until you fall asleep."

Rick made a good point. Jordan stood and put his nose to the door hole. He sniffed the air and smelt the gas. Rick was right. Gas was nearby. "Okay, I can smell it, but that doesn't help our situation."

"We can fuel the plane," Rick said with a smile. "We just have to find a way outta here."

Jordan sighed. "You still think we're gonna get outta here. The only way that's possible is they open the door. That's if they're stupid enough to check on us." He watched Rick look around the room.

"Or they're stupid enough to have a boarded roof," Rick's eyes checked out the ceiling structure. It was boarded with wood about ten feet over their heads.

Jordan looked up and saw what the ceiling was made of. "Sonovabitch," he muttered.

"The only problem is we don't have anything strong enough to break through it," Rick said while looking around the room.

"That's where you're wrong, rook," Jordan said and bent over the body of bones. He wrapped his hands around the skull, and the rat appeared. "Fuck," he fell back.

"Ha," Rick laughed. "You're scared of rats."

99

"I fuckin' hate rats," Jordan said, watching the rat scurry away. "You probably had one as a pet." He put his hands around the skull.

"Nah," Rick said nonchalantly. "I was more of a gerbil guy."

"Same thing," Jordan said as he began to tear the head loose.

"Actually, gerbils are more friendly, and they have—"

Jordan interrupted. "I don't wanna hear childhood stories of your pet best friend. Just help me pull this fuckin' skull loose." He struggled trying the remove the head from its neck. "This guy was made of fuckin' steel."

Rick grabbed the neck area of the body. "Place your hands under the chin and pull in the opposite direction on the count of three. One, two, three."

Jordan pulled back on the skull and fell back, detaching it from the neck. "Fuck," he sighed and stood with the head in his hands.

Rick watched Jordan as he held the skull. It was the perfect shot of a demon looking over a claimed soul. "You are the devil."

"In the flesh," Jodan stood on the stone seat. He was now tall enough to reach the ceiling and breakthrough using the skull. He beat several times against the wood, tiring out after each blow.

"Is it that hard to break through wood," Rick asked.

"You wanna try," Jordan replied and kept working. After a couple more hits, the wood began to give way. Finally, the job was complete. There was now an opening for them to climb through onto the roof. Jordan dropped the skull, hopped on the ledge, and pulled himself up.

Rick stood on the seat, hopped on the ledge, and pulled himself onto the roof. Jordan was already making his way down.

"There is enough kerosene to fly home after we're done," Jordan said as Rick hopped down.

"Done with what," Rick questioned.

Jordan smiled. "You ask too many questions." He spotted a rebel by himself smoking a cigarette. "Come on. I have a plan."

18 – Campsite

Snake looked at Bam and then over to Britt. Both men were watching her with hawk eyes and thought about what she would look like naked. Snake shook the thought from his mind and finished setting up the tent for the night. He wondered why they couldn't sleep in a nice hotel. Abel said it would be too dangerous if someone found out they had the diamond. He checked his watch and calculated the hours Abel and the others had been gone. He sighed. "It's been two hours."

Bam kept his eyes on Britt, and the woman didn't look back at him one time. The fact that she didn't pay him any mind pissed him off a bit. Was it because Silva was around, or did she just think he was ugly? Britt was playing with his emotions, and he wanted to tell her how he felt. Expressing himself would cause a stir with Silva, but he didn't give a damn. He'd kill Silva for Britt. That's how much he was attracted to her. They hadn't shared one moment, yet he was still ready to sacrifice someone's life for her. The way Britt's breasts were round and firmly propped up made his dick hard as if a baby had never sucked on her nipples. He didn't bother to hide it either. He wanted her to see what he was working with. He thought, *I should go over there and tell her how I feel.*

"Stop drooling over her," Snake said as he approached Bam.

"I saw you looking at her," Bam kept his eyes on Britt. She was sitting by the ocean with her feet in the water. Silva was inside the plane smoking weed, so he didn't notice them eyeing his girl. "Don't act like she doesn't get your Jimmy rock hard."

"And if she does, I wouldn't tell you," Snake said. "Anyway, she hasn't noticed us. She wants to be with Abel."

"Abel said she was for us," Bam said and picked up his bag. He unzipped it, pulled out a bottle of cologne, and doused himself with two squirts. "And Gina would kill her if she knew how Britt felt." *That's if I don't kill Gina first,* he thought.

"You brought cologne," Snake was shocked at Bam for bringing a bottle of smell good. He waved his hand in the air. Bam sprayed enough for them both. "I think you overdid it."

"I'm sure you would think that," Bam said and tossed the bag inside his tent. "You've never been with a woman in your life."

"Neither have you," Snake countered and looked over at Britt. It was beginning to get dark, and what was left of the sun rays seemed to only shine on her. Britt was his ideal woman. She

103

was perfect in every way, and he wanted to know everything about her. Abel was a lucky man. "At least I'm not afraid to admit it."

"Yeah, but that's about to change," Bam began to walk over to Britt, but Snake grabbed his arm. "Don't try to stop me."

"I'm not trying to stop you," Snake noticed something in the woods behind the plane. While he was watching Britt, he also watched Silva. There was definitely movement. "Someone's in the woods." He said in a whisper while keeping his eyes on the location.

"Nobody's in the woods," Bam jerked his arm away. "You're jealous because I'm gonna talk with her first."

"I'm not jealous, Bam," Snake said with meaning. "I'm serious." He pointed to the spot in the woods for Bam to see. "See for yourself. Right over there. I saw someone. I put it on my life." Snake held his hand on the watch. He was seconds away from activating it to signal Abel they were in trouble.

Bam was growing frustrated and looked in the direction Snake had pointed. He'd finally gained the confidence to speak with Britt, and Snake was ruining his moment. *Dammit,* he thought while walking toward the location. "I'll show you there's nothing in the woods, scaredy-pants."

"It's scaredy-cat," Snake corrected him. He followed behind Bam.

"Whatever," Bam muttered as he approached the plane. Silva was blowing the house down. The plane was smoked out, and he couldn't see anything on the inside. *No wonder he didn't see us watching his girl,* Bam thought.

"Let's get Silva outta the plane," Snake suggested. "He can help."

"He's high as a kite," Bam eyed Snake with a sarcastic expression on his face. "He won't be that much help. We're better off handling this alone. Besides, it's nothing anyway. You're just—"

"Airfae yadayk ealian," a rebel shouted as he appeared from the woods with an assault rifle.

"Shit," Bam fell back to the ground and began to crawl on his ass away from the threat.

"Airfae yadayk ealian," he shouted again as three more rebels appeared by his side. They all were toting assault rifles.

Snake held his hands high. "We don't want any trouble."

"What do they want," Bam asked, terrified.

The rebel aimed his weapon at Bam and fired a warning shot in the dirt. "Airfae yadayk ealian!"

"I don't understand," Bam was hysterical.

"He wants you to put your hands up," Snake told him.

"How do you know that's what he wants," Bam questioned.

The rebel fired another warning shot and moved closer.

"I took Arabic as an elective," Snake said. "Trust me or die."

Bam stood and cautiously held up his hands.

"La nurid mashakil," Snake said.

"What did you say," Bam asked.

"We don't want problems," Snake told Bam while waiting for a response.

"You speak my language," the rebel said in broken English.

"Yes," Snake answered. "I speak a little, not much."

The rebel smiled and looked behind Snake. "Tell the woman to come here."

Shit, Snake thought.

19 – Kane

"Where am I," I said as I walked through a field toward a cabin in the middle of nowhere. I saw a military jeep parked in the front as I got closer. I noticed a small Libyan flag painted on the side. I was in Africa somewhere, but how did I get here? I thought I was in a hotel lying next to Kim.

My first thought was to knock on the front door, but I decided to check things out beforehand. There was a window on the same side of the cabin I was on. I cautiously made my way over to see who was inside. As I approached the window, I could hear different voices. One of the voices sounded like my father's. There was no way it could be him because he was dead. I'm not trippin' that hard. Am I?

I wanted to see who sounded so close to the man I loved. My father meant everything to me. He showed me how to be a man and taught me things only a father could teach. I want to be just like him in every way. I'll raise my son the same way my father raised me.

I peered through the window, not trying to be noticed by the people inside. I saw a woman and two men. One of the men looked like a younger version of the General. But it couldn't be him. I was face to face with him in the warehouse. Maybe his son or another close relative? I couldn't see the other man's face because he had his back turned to me. I did notice his hair was done in a particular style, dreadlocks. Jamaican, I thought. While in thought, I caught a glimpse of the woman when she stood, and I couldn't believe my eyes. She looked similar to my mother, but I knew it wasn't her. I saw pictures of my mother when she was younger, and besides, my mother was with Jordan. She wouldn't come to Africa just to be in a cabin. That would be insane. Why would she keep that from me? The woman did resemble my mother in every way. They were the same height and build. Even her facial features were similar to my mother's. Wow, I thought. She could be her sister. The only problem was my mother didn't have any sisters. At least that's what she told me.

Suddenly, I was taken by surprise and staggered away from the window. I had to catch my breath. What I saw convinced me that my mind was playing tricks on me. The man who was speaking to the African soldier turned around and was the spitting image of my father. Every single detail I saw of my father in his younger days was right in front of me. It couldn't be, I questioned myself. My mind began to run wild. I just saw my father, I thought. I stood there, looking at the window as if it was some kind of time portal that sent me to the past. Again, I wondered. What was I doing here, and how did I get here? My father was dead, and my mother was with The Planner.

I felt a twitch in my hands and looked down. They were shaking uncontrollably. Faster than I've ever seen them move before. I balled my fists, trying to regain control of the nerves in my hands. I wanted to look through the window but couldn't bring myself to it. My legs were stuck in position. I couldn't move them at all. They felt paralyzed. I looked down at my feet and saw a pair of red and black Jordan 1s. What? I don't even own a pair in that colorway.

Never mind the shoes, and I focused on the window. I had to figure out what was going on. I took a deep breath and slowly walked over. Before looking through, I told myself no matter what I saw, my mother was with The Planner, my father was dead, and I don't own a fuckin' pair of red and black Jordan 1s. It was the only way to get my mind together. I peeped through the window and saw the man who resembled my father talking to the soldier. They were speaking about transporting weapons to a warehouse while the woman sat there and listened. After several minutes they agreed on the shipment and the payment amount. The man was a smuggler, just like my father.

The man walked the soldier to the door, and he left in the Jeep. I crept around to the front when the Jeep was far enough away from the cabin. The man stood on the porch until the Jeep disappeared in the distance. I wanted to speak to the man, so I revealed myself to him. Shockingly, the man didn't respond to me as if I wasn't standing blankly in front of him. "Can you hear me?" I asked as if the man was hard of hearing. He stood there, smiling and looking through me. He didn't know I was standing in front of him. I know he isn't blind, so why wasn't he responding to me?

I followed the man back into the house. I was the biggest thing there and very noticeable. Something had to be wrong because the woman paid me no mind either. The same reaction I got from the man. I stepped in front of her and shouted, "Can you see me?" and she didn't answer. What the hell was happening? I'm I trapped in some kind of ghost world?

The woman stepped in front of the man and said. "I love you."

The man held her close and repeated her words.

I watched them embrace for a moment, which angered me because I wasn't getting their attention.

The man pulled back and said. "The General will pay one hundred thousand per shipment."

"That's not enough for us to do what he's asking, Jar," the woman said.

Jar, I thought. There was no way I heard what I thought she said.

"Aayla," he said. "It's enough for now. When I take over, and it's only me running the smuggling trade. He'll pay more. We'll have enough to move to America, have children, and live a comfortable life without worries."

"Will we live in a big house," she asked with a smile.

I stood next to them, and still, they didn't notice me.

"We will, my love," he said.

"I want two boys," she said. "And we'll name them Kane and Abel."

"What," I said as if they could hear. "Kane and Abel." It blew my mind what the woman said. What the fuck was going on? Move to America and have children named after us. I'm losing it.

"No girls," he said. "Named after their beautiful mother?"

"No," she said. "I want strong men like their father. And when we get to America. I want to continue studying to become a doctor. I want to finish school there."

"We'll have enough money to pay for the best school," he said. "I promise you'll live the best life, Aayla. You mean the world to me."

"As do you to me," she said, and they embraced.

111

Suddenly, I heard another vehicle pull up to the cabin. I wanted to see who it could be, so I walked to the door and grabbed the knob. What? I couldn't open the door. My hand went through as if it was made of air. A lot of weird shit has happened, so I said fuck it and looked through the front window. A woman stepped out of a car and approached the house. What the . . . it was my mother!

"You have to hide," the man said. "Your sister is home."

I watched the woman hurry to the window and look through. "Noti's home? I thought she wouldn't be back until tomorrow from visiting mother?"

"I guess not," he said and hurried over. "I'll get her in the shower, and that will give me enough time to drive you back to Zuwarah."

"Okay," she said. "Promise you'll tell her that we want to be together?"

"I will," he kissed her as I heard footsteps on the porch. "Hurry, through the back."

I watched him rush her out the back door. Then, I turned my attention to the door as it opened.

"Jar," my mother called. "I'm home."

My father rushed over to her, appearing from the back room. "Honey." He lifted her from the ground. "You're home early."

She kissed him. "I love you."

"I love you more," he said. "How bout you take a shower and get settled. I have to go to the city and pick up a few things."

"Okay," she said. "Hurry back. We have some catching up to do."

"Okay, my love," he watched her hurry up the stairs.

I watched my father lie to my mother for the first time. What was even more important, he was cheating on her.

My father rushed out of the house when my mother turned on the shower. I followed him out of the house as he hurried the woman into the car and pulled away. Something told me I was being watched, so I turned around. No one was there and then . . . I looked up and saw my mother watching my father leave through the window. She had a sad look on her face, and then something happened that shocked me. Her eyes traveled down to me as if she could see me. She pressed a hand against the glass and said what appeared to be my name.

Suddenly, I wake up frantically. My chest was panting, and I noticed my surroundings. I was in the hotel room with Kim next to me. She was already up with a worried look on her face. I was dreaming, I thought.

Kim touched my shoulder. "Are you okay?"

"No," I told her, trying to calm down.

"What is it," she said. "You kept saying, Aayla, while you were asleep. Who is she?"

I looked Kim dead in the eyes and said. "My aunt."

20 – Jordan

"This way," Jordan led the way behind the small room they were captive inside. He slid against the back of the shed and peeped around the corner. He scanned the area and noticed the rebel was the only person on guard.

"Is he alone," Rick asked, sliding next to Jordan.

"Shut up before you get yourself killed," Jordan whispered while keeping his eyes on the soldier.

"Wha . . .," Rick whispered. "And I guess you'll somehow survive without me."

"That's the plan," Jordan said.

"Sure it is," Rick tried to look around Jordan to view the scene.

"What are you doing, stupid," Jordan bumped against Rick, trying to move him back.

"I wanna see what's going on," Rick said.

"I told you I have a plan," Jordan eyed Rick.

"Like in the room back there," Rick countered. "I think it's wise I have a look."

Rick wants to be in charge, Jordan thought after seeing the serious look on his face. He signed with a slight nod. "Ok, you got it, rook." Jordan moved back along the wall to let Rick move ahead.

Rick stepped around Jordan and peeped around the edge of the wall. The rebel Jordan had mentioned was smoking a cigarette by himself. He scanned the area and didn't see anyone coming or going from the main building in the city. Suddenly, he felt a forcefully push on his back, and he stumbled wildly out into the open where the rebel could see him. "You sonova . . .," before he could get the words out, Jordan was gone. Rick looked toward the back wall and didn't see Jordan anywhere. *Sonovabitch set me up,* he thought.

"A tataharak, 'aw sa' utliq alnaar," the rebel held his gun on Rick.

Rick quickly turned his attention to the rebel, forgetting about Jordan. He couldn't understand what the soldier had said, but he figured it had something to do with don't move, or I'll shoot. *Dammit,* he thought while slowly holding up his hands. Jordan had gotten one over on him, and it was a good one. *This is where it all ends, Rick.* Jordan and Adrian didn't need him because they had already made it to Africa. There wasn't a need for him anymore. Honestly, he'd thought they would've tossed him from the plane upon entering the country. At this point, Rick was grateful for being alive.

"Where is your partner," the rebel shouted in broken English. "The black man!"

As the soldier cautiously eased forward, Rick tried to develop a plan. If the rebel came in arms reach, maybe he could take the gun.

"Where is the black—" suddenly, someone grabbed the rebel from behind, cutting him off.

Rick's eyes grew to the size of almonds when he saw Jordan appear and grab the soldier by the neck. He watched Jordan strangle the rebel until his eyes rolled to the back of his head. The fight was over, and Jordan released hold of the rebel's neck, and he dropped to the ground. Rick couldn't believe what he'd seen. Jordan used him as bait. At that moment, another thought ran across his mind. Jordan still needed him. Why else would Jordan save him when he could've easily escaped on his own?

After the rebel fell to the ground, Jordan picked up his AK-47. He looked the rifle over and made sure it was ready to fire. He smirked and held the weapon on Rick. "Bang. You're dead, rook."

Jordan pretended to shoot Rick, and for a moment. Rick thought Jordan would kill him after he aimed the weapon at him. Rick played it cool as if Jordan wouldn't dare shoot him. "Stop fuckin' joking before you get us both killed. The others are still around, and we need to get at least two barrels of kerosene back to the plane."

Jordan lowered the rifle. "That won't happen without them noticing us. We have to travel through the city with the barrels to get back to the plane. The same way we came in, we have to go out."

Rick scanned around the area. "How many of them were they?"

"At least ten," Jordan replied. "We need Adrian's help."

Rick let out a chuckle. "How hard was that for you to say?"

"Very," Jordan said, looking down at the rebel. The soldier was close in size to him. He began to come up with a way for them to escape the city without being noticed. "Let's drag this guy out of the open and behind the shed."

"Do you have another genius plan in mind that would possibly put my life in danger," Rick asked sarcastically.

"Any plan I come up with will put your life in danger," Jordan told him while reaching for the rebel's right leg. "Does that make you feel better?"

Rick grabbed the left leg. "Somehow, it does. I can't expect anything from you to be rational." They began to drag the rebel behind the shed.

"Well, we got this far, so I guess we're doing alright," Jordan said and released the rebel.

"What now," Rick let go once the rebel was out of sight. "What's the big plan?"

Jordan had already begun to strip down and then worked on the soldier. He padded him down and then took off the soldier's attire.

"What are you doing?" Rick asked curiously.

Jordan slipped on the rebel's pants. "Putting your life in danger.

21 – Abel

"After all these years," Abel said while sitting in a fold-out chair for patients. "I have an aunt that I wasn't aware of."

Aayla began to wrap Abel's ribs with bandages after applying special medication that would allow them to heal faster. "I knew this day would come."

Abel thought about telling Aayla why he came to Africa. Aayla told him what happened between her and his parents. Jar was in love with both sisters and used Aayla to get to the General. Aayla had overheard the General conversing about bringing more weapons into the country at a bar. Jar was in the smuggling business and wanted to find an African connection. Aayla's beauty and persuasive ways got Jar the meeting he needed. Jar became a millionaire after dealing with the General. After a few successful runs, Jar and Noti moved to the United States, leaving Aayla in Zuwarah. She traveled back to Mizdah, although she never heard from Jar or Noti again. Jar betrayed Aayla and ran off with her older sister.

Aayla saw the look on Abel's face. He didn't appear worried but deep in thought. "What is on your mind?" No one else was in the room with them. Gina, Oyoo, and a rebel soldier remained in the lobby of the building, waiting for them to finish. Aayla didn't allow anyone in the room while attending to her patients, so they had privacy.

Abel sat up straight when Aayla finished bandaging his wounds. He sighed. Something about Aayla made him feel like they were the same. Not because they were family. He felt another kind of connection with her as if they were one and the same. "Jar is dead, and your sister is in a mental hospital."

Aayla stood next to Abel, looked him in the eyes, and said. "Good, I wish I could thank the man who killed him. And Noti renounced us as sisters the day she ran off with the man I loved."

Abel met Aayla's stare. "Then you should be thanking me."

Aayla smirked. "My nephew is more like me than I thought."

"More than you know," Abel responded while putting on his shirt.

"You found the black notebook," Aayla said.

"I did," Abel finished dressing and felt better now that his ribs had been treated.

"I gave Jar the notebook as a gift many years ago," she said. "The notebook is the key. Do you have it with you?"

"No," Abel said evenly. "It's back at the camp."

"There are numbers at the bottom of several pages that appear to be page numbers," Aayla walked to the cabinets and opened them. "Did you notice the pages without numbers?"

Abel thought about it for a moment. He'd studied the notebook for hours and saw the pages without numbers on the bottom. He didn't think anything of it at the time, and it never crossed his mind that the numbers meant something important. "I did. What does it mean?"

"The missing numbers form the code to Jar's underground bunker," Aayla handed Abel a green substance. "Drink it. It will help with the pain."

Abel opened the container and smelled the substance. It didn't smell tasty, but he downed it anyway. He handed the empty container back to Aayla. "Underground bunker. I thought Jar secured his money in a safe in one of his warehouses?"

Aayla smiled. "The bunker is hidden in a warehouse in Mizdah. I am the only one who knows the location of the bunker. Jar didn't trust anyone. I saw the floorplan when he was asleep, and Noti was away. He was secretive, and I wanted to know what he was planning. That's why we need the notebook."

Abel slightly shook his head. Aayla was giving him valuable information about Jar, and he decided to let her in on why he was in Africa. "I have the diamond."

"There's only one diamond that matters," Aayla said. "The African Black Diamond."

"I'm here to see the General," Abel said truthfully. "In return, I want everything Jar once possessed turned over to me."

Aayla chuckled. "The General will kill you once the diamond is in his possession." She lied to get Abel on her side. Nothing she did was in favor of the General. "I can offer you something better."

"What could a doctor offer me that the General couldn't obliterate," Abel said seriously.

"You can take my place," Aayla said. "And I will take you to the bunker."

"I could've become a doctor in the United States," Abel said. "Even if you show me to the bunker. I couldn't get the money out of the country without the General opposing a fight."

"That's where you're wrong, Abel," Aayla said. "You underestimate your aunt. I'm not just a doctor. I am the leader of the largest rebel army in Africa."

Abel's eyes grew wide. He was in shock after what Aayla had told him. She was the rebel army leader and wanted him to take her place. This was more than he could ever ask for. He'd have his very own army. *Why would she do this,* he thought. A genius would not be a genius if they didn't question everything in front of them. Abel thought about how the soldier got scared once he learned he was Jar's son. Aayla must have struck fear in their heart. It wasn't Jar but Aayla who controlled them. "Why would you do this for me? And what would you do once I'm the leader? Remain a simple doctor?"

"No," Aayla said. "I would go back to Jamaica and take over as queen. Your grandmother is dying, and she is the queenpin of this operation. How do you think Jar got his start? As queen, I will control Jamaica's smuggling trade. You will be my lieutenant here in Africa as I am to her. We will grow, and one day, nephew. You will be the king."

"Grandmother," he muttered. Not only did he have an aunt, but a grandmother as well. Everything was happening fast and was almost too much to take in at once. Aayla was letting him know who he really was and the family he belonged to. Abel was born into a criminal empire. He figured it's why he always thought like one. It ran in his veins. From his grandmother down to him. He was vicious like his mother's side of the family. Every once of anger and criminal acts came from them. He wanted to know more about his grandmother and how the operation worked, but before he could ask another question. His watch sounded and lit up red.

22 – Kane

"What are you talking about," Kim sat next to me with a worried look. "You don't have an aunt."

I sighed, happy the dream was over. There was a lot to take in from what I saw. My father cheated on my mother with a woman named Aayla, who I now think is my aunt. My mother didn't mention anything about having a sister. The dream felt real as if I was there reliving the situation with them. "I think I do."

"Your father wouldn't cheat on your mother," Kim said. "And if you have an aunt, your mother would've told you."

"I know my father was a family man," I turned to the side and looked Kim in the eyes. "But he was also hiding things from us. Before his death, I didn't know he was a smuggler. Look where we're at? My mother is here in Africa, looking for his headquarters with The Planner. We're in this situation because of him. My mother loved him dearly and would do anything for him, even if that meant erasing her sister."

Kim sighed as if she was having a hard time comprehending the situation. "Okay, let's say you do have an aunt. In the dream, your father took Aayla to Zuwarah. Do you think that's where she lives?"

"Maybe," I said. "She could've been staying there at the time, but that was twenty years ago. After my father left for America, I don't think there was any reason for her to stay. She could've gone back home to Jamaica."

Kim's eyes traveled downwards for a second. I could tell she was deep in thought. When she locked eyes with me again, she said. "Let's go to Zuwarah and see if she's there?"

I slowly shook my head no. "Nah, we have to get to Mizdah. Finding my mother is more important. We could be wasting time chasing a ghost. Why would she stay in Africa anyway?" At that moment, what I said, hit me square in the chin. It was the reason I had the dream in the first place. It was the reason my mother didn't want me to follow her. My mother needed killers. The Planner and Adrian were the perfect candidates. Those two would do anything for money, even if it meant working with the enemy.

I'd zoned out for a moment, and when I came back to reality, Kim was eyeing me. "You figured it out, didn't you?"

126

I shook my head yes at her. "Aayla was in love with my father, and if she knew about the headquarters. That would give her a reason to stay. Aayla wanted my father to get more money from the General in my dream, but he didn't want to be greedy. What if Aayla wanted to replace my father?"

"What do you mean," Kim asked. "You said they were in love."

"True," I said. "But what I mean is, what if she wanted to be in his place, working with the General, running the operation my father built. After Aayla realized my father wouldn't be with her. It broke her heart, and maybe she didn't take it well. A broken heart could be dangerous, especially if that person is vindictive."

"I see," Kim said. "Aayla wants to be in control. Do you think she found your father's headquarters?"

"There's a possibility she's running the place," I said seriously.

"The General wouldn't let a Jamaican woman run a smuggling business on his land," Kim sighed. "That's not possible . . . right?"

"I think money runs the land," I said, looking her in the eyes. "If the business is profitable. There's a chance, but there is a chance she's working with someone else."

"What do you mean?"

"If not with the General," I leaned back against the bed to get my thoughts together. "Maybe there's someone like my father or perhaps a group. Let's assume the General didn't agree to her payment request or doesn't want to work with a woman. Aayla would need an army to operate."

"The rebels," Kim spoke up.

I turned to her attention and looked at her worriedly. Suppose Aayla gained control of the rebels or is somehow involved with them. What would that mean for my mother if Aayla found out she was in Africa? "Let's hope not."

I heard Kim murmur, "A woman in charge of the rebels."

I got up from bed and headed for the bathroom.

"Where are you going," she called after me. "Are you okay?"

"I'm fine," I assured her. "Just need to splash some water on my face. My head is all over the place." I opened the door and didn't bother to close it. I wanted Kim to see what I was doing so she wouldn't worry. I turned on the faucet and listened to the water run down the drain, wondering if I was losing my mind. My dreams are not just vivid images of my past or future. They're signs that should be paid attention to. I don't even think they're dreams anymore because they feel like an alternate reality. This one wasn't any different. I was there, living in the past with my parents, the General, and my aunt.

"Kane," I heard Kim's voice.

I snapped back to reality. I could hear the water running down the drain again. I'd zoned out, looking at myself in the mirror. "Yeah."

"You're just staring at yourself in the mirror," she said. "Don't worry yourself, baby. Come back to bed."

"I'm good, baby," I lied. I wasn't good at all, and I didn't feel good either. I splashed water on my face and turned off the faucet. Before I left the bathroom, I looked in the mirror once more. I thought about my life being a lie. Since my father's death, I've discovered all kinds of secrets. And my life has been in danger ever since. I used to think my life was perfect and nothing could go wrong. That was my parents providing a false livelihood for an ignorant child. Now that my eyes are open, I can see the danger they actually put me in. Even if I was still blind to what they had done, I understand why they did it.

23 – The General

The General sat back and watched Abrafo torture the traitor. He could already smell the burnt aroma from the rebel's feet. The General was enjoying every second of it. There was nothing like hearing an enemy who thinks he's a soldier cry out for forgiveness. The bottom of the traitor's feet wore black spots where the fire made contact. This type of torture was worse than walking across hot coal. At least you'd know when the pain would end in that situation. After ten minutes, the General sighed and stood after turning a soldier back into a regular boy. "Abrafo."

Abrafo heard the General call his name from behind. The lighter chimed shut, momentarily ending the rebel's cries. Abrafo stood and backed away, never taking his cold eyes off the traitor. This was only the beginning process. No words would come from the rebel until near death. Most prisoners would hold out until then or a family member, such as the capture of their child. In some cases, a traitor's pride would get in the way and bring them to a slow death. In the end, Abrafo had never left anyone he's tortured alive.

The General stood in front of the rebel and looked down into his swollen eyes. A devilish smirk formed across his face. "Who is the one ordering the raid of my camps?"

The traitor's heart rate was rapid. Sweat poured down his face as if water had been dumped over his head. His chest heaved deep breaths of air. The pain was nothing like anything he'd ever felt. Nothing compared to the experience at hand, and overcoming this predicament meant death. There wasn't anything that could affect him emotionally—no family, brothers or sisters, wife, or children to care for after the war. His parents were among the many casualties who stood against the president's law. They died when he was ten. Since then, he's been on his own. If he died today, his death would mean nothing, and sadly . . . that's how he wanted it.

The General waited for a response that never came. He collapsed his hands behind his back and patiently waited for the traitor to speak. The rebel struggled to keep his head from bobbling up and down as though staying awake was difficult. The General decided to carry on with torturing the man in front of him. "Abrafo."

Abrafo stepped forward as the General backed away. The sound of the lighter flicking open terrified the rebel. The traitor began to shout and fight with the two soldiers keeping him at bay. "A man with nothing to say is a man at peace."

"No," the traitor cried. He could see the shape of a man standing before him—the exact figure who set fire to his feet.

"The pain will pass," Abrafo got closer as he spoke in an even tone. "You are a man at peace. Are you not?" the lieutenant desired to see how far he could go without harming the rebel before losing control.

"Please," the rebel held his head up at Abrafo. "No more. I'm . . . sorry for what I've done." His head dropped down toward his lap.

"The General asked you a question," Abrafo said as he gripped the traitor's chin and lifted his head upward. "Not I."

"Please," the rebel pleaded.

"Shhh . . .," Abrafo slid a finger over the rebel's mouth. "I won't burn your feet." He shut the lighter and placed it inside his jacket pocket. Abrafo released his chin and left the tent. He returned with a small table he retrieved from another tent within seconds. Abrafo set it in front of the traitor. "I want to show you something you should get familiar with." He revealed a weapon. "Can you see what I have for you?"

The General was well aware of Abrafo's intentions. What was about to happen to the traitor excited him. A part of unbearable torture that takes away from a man's body. The makeup of a man or a woman. A state of mind in which psychology interrupts your brain's behavior. Your way of thinking no longer exists in your mind because of the pain. Every single nerve in your body erupts, and an explosion of information translates to the brain that something isn't right. After that occurs is when you understand that Abrafo is not just your tormentor . . . but the devil.

The rebel felt his head lift in an upward position. He was too exhausted to see the object. It appeared long and shiny. He could see a reflection of himself in the object. At least he thought it was him staring back. He heard the man speaking but didn't hear what was said clearly. Suddenly, he felt his arm jerked and placed on a sturdy platform.

"Remember," the rebel listened to the man. "You are a man at peace."

"Ah . . .," the rebel let out a horrific yell and swiftly retracted his right arm. Pain shot through his arm like a lightning bolt splitting a tree in half. He tried to stand, but the soldiers forced him down. There wasn't anywhere to run. Blood shot from his hand onto his already blood sweaty face. He went into shock and began to shake uncontrollably as if he was experiencing a seizure.

"Abrafo," the General called to the lieutenant. "One at a time."

"Please accept my apology General," Abrafo turned to face him.

The General nodded. "Carry on, lieutenant."

Abrafo used the machete to scrap four of the traitor's fingers off the table. He then held the machete against the rebel's neck. "Be still," he ordered. "Or I'll cut your throat." He turned his attention to the soldier on the right. "Wrap his hand."

The soldier picked up the shirt they took off the traitor and wrapped his hand tightly. He made sure it was secure before moving back into position.

The rebel couldn't slow down his breathing. If saying nothing meant death, he was ready to die. There wasn't anything more he'd wish for. But, the General wouldn't let him off so easy. How long could he last before it came to an end? He thought about if they would keep him alive? The General wanted the name of the group's leader. Was giving up his comrade's location and, more importantly, their superior worth an accelerated death?

Abrafo pointed to the soldier on the left. "Place his arm on the table."

The soldier did what he was told after a brief struggle.

The rebel turned into a wild man as the soldier forced his left arm down on the table and held out his hand.

"No," the rebel yelled loud enough for the entire campsite to hear.

Abrafo grabbed the index finger and laid the blade across it. This had to be a slow and cautious process so he wouldn't detach any of the other fingers by mistake. That would anger the General. The blade was previously sharpened for precise cuts such as this one. A small amount of pressure applied over the top, and the rebel would need a new finger.

"Ah," the rebel cried at the top of his lungs. He couldn't retract his hand this time because the soldier kept it in place.

"Again," the General said calmly from behind.

Abrafo scraped the finger off the table and prepared another.

"Aayla," the rebel said in a shout before dropping his head. He felt ashamed after giving the General what he wanted. The pain was overwhelming, and his mind couldn't endure it anymore. "Aayla is the person you seek," he said, heaving and frightened that he'd lose another finger. "Please kill me."

Aayla, the General thought back to where he'd heard the name before. "A woman," he said to himself. His thoughts were interrupted as he watched Abrafo scrap another finger off the table.

24 – Left Alone

Noti thought about what Rick said as she watched him walk away with Jordan. She got involved with two very dangerous men. There was no way she could turn back the hands of time. She had two options. They would kill her if she didn't come through on their agreement. The second option was non-negotiable. They would bury her six feet deep. *Use the resources around you to make a weapon;* Rick's words rang out in her head.

Noti searched around the area for something useful but couldn't find anything before Adrian got back on the plane. Adrian would notice any suspicious activity, so she decided to hold off. She sat down in the same seat. She didn't want Adrian to suspect wrongdoing, or he'd kill her. She had to come up with a plan. Not just any plan. A maneuver that would bring Adrian to her side for good and against Jordan in a worst-case scenario.

Adrian didn't sit in the polite's seat. Instead, he sat directly across from her. Noti stared at him for a moment but not for too long. She looked away as their eyes met. "Are you watching me?"

"Of course," Adrian responded.

"Why," Noti looked at him from the corner of her eyes. "I'm not dangerous."

Adrian snickered. "You're not dangerous. I beg to differ."

Noti noticed Adrian's eyes didn't move off her for a second. "What could I do to a man like you?"

"Look at where I'm at," Adrian held up his hands as if to show her what she didn't know already. "In Africa."

"How does that make me dangerous by you being in Africa," Noti sat up straight to face him.

"I'm here without pay," he said. "You convinced me to be here without a single payment. That makes you a dangerous woman."

"It was your brother who convinced you, not me," she said.

"But it was your words that convinced him that he needed my help," Adrian got a good look at Noti and noticed how beautiful she was for the first time. Every time their eyes met, she'd look away. She kept eye contact with him the entire time he spoke. "That couldn't have been easy to do. Jordan and I have been on bad terms for years. And now, all of a sudden. Big brother needs my help." He cracked a smile and shook his head. "What did you do to him?"

Noti looked into Adrian's eyes, and they didn't appear cold as before. The man across from her was taking in her beauty. Noti knew when a man wanted her. She had gotten those kinds of lustful eyes on several occasions. She quickly came up with a plan. Rick told her to get a weapon, and she was gonna use the most dangerous weapon on the plane. Noti stood and walked seductively toward Adrian as she said. "You wanna know what I did to him?" She stopped in front of him and lifted her right leg, leveling it with his head. She positioned her clit in front of his face.

"What are you doing," Adrian didn't move. Noti was close enough to his face that his nose was in her crotch.

"Are you hungry," Adrian tried to move, and she forced him down by placing her leg over his shoulder and leaning forward. "I asked if you were hungry?" She slowly lifted her dress and pulled her satin-laced panties to the side, revealing a nicely shaven clitoris. She leaned closer and could feel him breathing on it. She hasn't been with a man since her husband. This was something she'd thought would never happen. Jar would want her to survive, and that's what she was doing. Abel came to Africa and would try to take everything they had left. Her own son would kill her to find the headquarters as he did with his father. Jordan was a maniac, and the General was not far off. She needed protection, and Adrian was it.

Adrian felt Noti grab the back of his head, forcing it forward. His nose touched first. *I asked if you were hungry?* He heard her say. "Yes," Adrian felt helpless. Noti was beautiful, and it's been a while since he'd been with an attractive woman of her stature.

"Then eat," she said seductively. She felt Adrian licking around her clit and sticking his tongue inside. She instantly got wet as he worked his magic. She closed her eyes as her legs began to vibrate. It was an amazing sensation throughout her body. For the moment, nothing else mattered. She held the back of Adrian's head, pressing it against her clit. His tongue was more than pleasurable. She began to climax as he created waves with his tongue. "Um . . .," she moaned. She had a visual of Jar in her mind as she came. She pulled back, sat on Adian's lap, and started kissing his neck. "Do you want me," she grinded against Adrian's manhood.

"Yes," he answered. There was something about Noti that he couldn't resist. He needed her. He lifted her to unbuckle his pants. His manhood was free and at attention. "I want you."

"You will protect me until this is over," she said while sitting on his manhood and grinding down on it. She could feel his rock-hard shaft. She was tempted to insert it but stopped.

"I will," he said, lost for words.

Noti reached down and stroked his soldier. "I need you to promise?" She rubbed it against her clit and inserted the head just enough to torture him.

"I promise," he said while kissing her on the neck. "I'll protect you."

Noti smiled before opening her eyes. "Good," she said and stood. She fixed her clothes.

"Wha . . .," Adrian was confused.

"I'll give you what you want when this is over," she returned to her seat and eyed him.

"You can't leave me like this," he pleaded. "I promised already."

"Then keep me alive," she said.

Adrian fixed his clothes, thinking about how she played him.

Noti noticed the angry look on his face. "I promise you can have me."

"Is this how you convinced my brother," he said.

"No," She answered truthfully. "He's different from you."

"How," Adrian asked.

Noti smiled. "The only thing he cares about is money."

25 – Abel

"What is that," Aalya asked, looking at Abel's wristwatch. The watch resembled a compass with a red arrow pointing northwest. An alarm sound came from the device that appeared to be a regular watch at first glance.

"Trouble," Abel told his aunt. "It's a tracking device that'll give coordinates toward anyone who presses this button." Abel pointed to a tiny button on the side of the device.

"You all have one," Aayla asked as Abel prepared to leave.

"Yes," he informed her.

"Genius," Aayla whispered. After speaking with Abel for thirty minutes, she knew that he was next in line to take her place. There wasn't a single soldier she's met who was more intelligent than her nephew. "Abel—"

Before Aayla could finish, Gina burst through the door. "We have to go. There's trouble at the camp." Gina didn't give a damn what was going on at the campsite. Bam was expendable even though she desired to be the one he saw before his last breath. Snake was a bit different. Abel would be hurt if his best friend was to die. She also knew they would need his help to finish the job. What mattered most was not leaving Abel alone with Aayla. The last thing Gina wanted was for Aayla to convince Abel that she was no longer needed. Gina thought of the worse outcome in any situation. She was still on edge about Aalya claiming to be Abel's long-lost aunt.

"Stop," the soldier shouted while holding his gun on Gina.

Gina didn't even turn around to acknowledge the soldier as she spoke. "You have five seconds to get that gun off me." She slowly reached for her waistband. "Four."

Aalya noticed Gina reaching for her waistband. *She has a weapon,* Aayla thought. What else could it be? "Stop," Aayla held up her hand for the soldier to see. "There's no need for violence. Abel is our leader. We will help resolve your problem."

Gina was shocked when she heard what Aalya said. *Leader,* she thought. There was only one explanation. Aayla gave Abel control of the rebels.

The soldier's eyes journeyed past Gina. He saw the look in Aalya's eyes and lowered his weapon. He looked at Abel, his new leader. "I apologize."

Abel acknowledged the soldier with a simple nod before turning to Aalya. "We have to go."

"What do you need from me," Aayla asked.

"We have to travel through the woods toward the sea," Abel said. "We'll need a vehicle if possible and a soldier or two."

"Ok," Aayla led the way into the lobby. She ordered two soldiers to accompany Abel for support. "There is a jeep around back you can take." She walked up to Abel and grabbed his shoulders. "Be safe, nephew. I'll be here when you return."

Abel sighed and nodded at his aunt. He couldn't help but think how similar Aayla looked to his mother as they switched faces.

Gina stepped next to them and said. "Thank you for your help." She smiled at Aayla and then looked at Abel. "I'll see you out back." She left out of the door.

Oyoo stepped forward. "Be safe," he touched Abel on the shoulder. He noticed Abel's facial expression. "The warzone is no place for me. I can hardly fight a simple cold." He smiled. "We'll continue our mission once you return, son of Jar."

Aayla guided Abel to the back door. Oyoo stayed close behind them. She stopped just before the threshold and said. "I need you and the notebook back here safely."

"Don't worry," Abel said. "I can handle myself."

"If the General is there," Aayla said sincerely. "Run."

"Not without the notebook," Abel said seriously. "He'll have to kill me."

143

Aayla smiled. Abel was ready to be a leader. She wanted to test his courage. He wasn't afraid to die, which she valued most. After spending time with Abel, she realized he was nothing like Jar. Jar was a man of peace. Abel was a man of genius and intimidation, exactly what the army would need when she was gone.

26 – Jordan

Jordan dressed in the rebel's clothes. Rick picked up the rebel's weapon while he was occupied. Jordan reached for the gun. "Give me that."

"What," Rick had a curious look on his face. "So you can murder me out in the middle of nowhere."

"If I was gonna murder you," Jordan sighed. "I would've done it already." Rick would've been correct under different circumstances. For now, he needed Rick to get out of this predicament.

Rick pointed the gun in Jordan's face. "You're a funny guy."

"You're even funnier," *You have about three seconds before I change my mind,* Jordan thought. He had to block out The Planner from doing something he'd regret. Once they got the kerosene back to the plane. Rick would be a dead man. Surprisingly, he needed Rick until this point. Luckily, he decided not to toss Rick into the sea on their trip over.

Rick smirked. *I could end this right here. It'll be over for The Planner,* he thought. The only problem was they were in Africa. Rick wouldn't have to decide on taking out Jordan in the U.S. Here he actually needed his help to survive. The rifle in his hands wouldn't be enough. Eventually, he would run out of ammo. If there were another way to avoid working with Jordan and his brother, he would do it. His main concern was making it back to America alive with Mrs. Simmons. "What's the plan?" Rick flipped the gun forward, handing it over to Jordan.

Jordan took the gun and muttered. "Asshole."

"You're not in your feelings, are you," Rick had a sarcastic expression.

"I don't have feelings," Jordan said while checking over the weapon. He pulled out the clip. *Full,* he thought. He popped it back in, loaded the gun, and looked down the iron sights. The alignment of the sights and the barrel wasn't perfect but would work.

"Come on, Rambo," Rick interrupted. "What's the plan?"

Jordan lowered the weapon. *I fucking hate this guy*, he thought. *What's the plan? What's the plan? Oh, no. Jordan, don't kill me.* He mocked in his mind. "We want to avoid the stone building." He looked toward the small town. "We'll work our way around the outside perimeter of the wall. Take out the two guards watching the front. Regroup at the plane and develop a plan to get the kerosene."

"Wait," Rick said worriedly. "Take out the guards in the front? I don't have a weapon."

Jordan searched the ground and found what he was looking for. He picked up the item and handed it to Rick.

"What the fuck," Rick said. "A rock? You trying to get me killed?" Rick thought about throwing the rock at Jordan's head and taking back the rifle.

"That's a nice size rock," Jordan said sarcastically.

"Fuck you," Rick dropped the rock. "I had enough of your bullshit."

Jordan chuckled. "Just following closely and stay low. If you make a sound, I'll kill you before they will. When we get to the front of the wall, I'll lure out the first guy, and we'll take him out. The second guard will react quickly, so be alert."

"What if the first guy set off an alarm," Rick asked. "Then what?"

"Well . . . since you dropped the rock," Jordan said seriously. "Run in the opposite direction away from me."

"Right," Rick said. "Make sure you don't shoot me in the back."

"Don't worry. I'll try my best." Jordan left the conversation there and led the way toward the wall. The wall was made of stone and was around ten feet high that traveled around the entire perimeter of the small town. Jordan stood over six feet tall, so making it over the wall wouldn't be a problem. He strapped the rifle over his shoulder, crouched down, and held out his hands to give Rick a boost.

"I can make the jump," Rick stood around the same height as Jordan but on the heavier side. He wasn't fat but ate more than enough doughnuts.

Jordan shrugged and stood. He watched Rick take a step back and prepare for the first attempt. Rick was taking his sweet time, and it frustrated Jordan. "C'mon already."

"Shut up," Rick said while rubbing his hands together. He had to get mentally prepared. "Here we go," he muttered while sprinting. He got within five feet of the wall, jumped, and reached for the edge. It appeared Rick would make the jump but fell short and smacked into the wall hard. He fell on his back and held his chest. "Fuck."

Jordan chuckled, walked over to Rick, and stood over him. "You stupid fuck. White men can't jump. You didn't see the movie?" He held out his hand.

Rick slapped it away. "I don't need your help."

Jordan sighed, watching Rick get on his feet.

"Of course, I saw the movie," Rick brushed himself off. "It was bullshit. White men can jump."

"Name one," Jordan said.

"Blake Griffin," Rick shook his head as if he'd won the argument.

"What," Jordan said. "He's half black."

"You didn't say he had to be one hundred percent," Rick said.

"Ok, smart guy," Jordan crouched and held out his hands. "You're gonna need half my help."

"Funny," Rick said. "Get outta my way, dick head. I got this." He took off toward the wall and leaped forward with everything ounce of strength left in his legs. *White men can jump,* he thought. Rick swore he heard his shirt rip as he stretched out his arm. His fingertips gripped the top of the wall surface just enough to hold up his weight. The jump wasn't pretty, but he made it. He hung on the edge, unable to lift himself over to the opposite side. The first attempt drained his energy after colliding with the wall. *White men can jump,* he thought. *Fuck you, Jordan.*

"Congratulation," Jordan gave Rick an unreal round of applause. "I didn't know they made Thorogoods with springs." He leaned against the wall casually next to Rick.

Rick grunted, trying to keep hold of the edge. His shoes slipped off the stone surface as he tried to climb over. "Dammit, you're gonna sit there and watch me struggle."

149

Jordan shrugged. "I thought you were Blake Griffin a minute ago." He crossed his arms over his chest.

"I made it didn't I," Rick sounded winded. "Who said anything about climbing over the damn thing."

"Like I said," Jordan taunted. "White men can't jump." He took his sweet time to help. He grabbed the soles of Rick's shoes and boosted him upward.

Rick had enough leverage to hoist himself over the wall. He made a sound an eighty-year-old would make trying to do something difficult involving strength. His right leg was nearly over when he saw Jordan leap up the wall from a standing position, grab the edge, and pull himself over easily. *What the fuck,* Rick thought.

"Hey," Jordan said after landing safely on the opposite side. "What's taking so long, rook."

Rick climbed over and slid down the wall cautiously, trying not to break his legs. He bent over, grabbed his knees, and took a deep breath. "I'm not young as I used to be."

"It's not because you're old," Jordan said.

"Because I'm white, right," Rick looked up at Jordan.

"You said it, not me," Jordan shrugged. He scanned the outside wall to make sure it was clear.

Rick was pissed that Jordan jumped the wall with ease. It was a piece of cake for him. What made matters worse was

Jordan was older than him. Rick began to doubt himself. *Maybe it's because I'm white,* he thought. He hated the thought of Jordan being right about something so stupid. "Fucking movie." He muttered.

"C'mon," Jordan called to Rick. He focused ahead on the first guard, pacing back and forth on the left side of the wall. The guard was making it too easy for him. Jordan studied that rebel's every move like a predator does its prey. He thought the thugs back home would be a more formidable challenge than the soldier. The Planner reminded him that things aren't as simple as they appear. The rebel lived a life of violence. Every day was a fight for survival. They called back home the jungle, but this was the jungle.

Rick stood next to Jordan and spotted the guard. "What are you thinking?"

"I'm thinking about killing you," Jordan said sarcastically. "Shut up and follow my lead, rook." Jordan crept along the wall until he was a few feet away from the guard. He posted on the outer edge where the rebel soldier would stop and survey the area. Jordan waited patiently for the rebel to reach the point of attack. He readied as the soldier approached without noticing him. Suddenly, Jordan felt an unexpected bump in his back and stumbled into the open. He quickly regained his footing, but it was too late. He was looking down the barrel of the rebel's rifle.

27 – Kane

I tossed and turned for the rest of the night. Kim fell back asleep five minutes after I returned to bed. Even though I kept my eyes shut, I couldn't sleep. The dream I had of my parents and the possibility of having an aunt bothered me. I'm unsure if Aayla is my mother's sister or not, but it's clear something is very wrong. Why else would I have a vision come to me as evident? I rolled over and checked the time on the clock sitting on the table. It was only seven in the morning. The crew was still in bed. It was a long night, and they ended it the same way I did with Kim. We had a good time, and everyone got lit. I wanted to knock on their room door to see if anyone would answer, but I expected no one would be up this early. I took a deep breath and just stared at the ceiling for another hour until I heard Kim.

"Hey, baby," Kim rolled over and looked at me. "You're up early."

"Yeah," I said as if I had woken up at the same time as her. "I've been up for about thirty minutes." I didn't want her to worry because I couldn't sleep. If I'd told her the truth, she'd question if I was ok. I think about what she went through and how fast she recovered. The doctor told me Kim needs to be stress-free. So if I had to tell her a few white lies to get her from worrying, that's what I'll do for her health. She came to Africa with me, chasing after The Planner. That was enough danger to deal with, and I feel bad she's in this situation because of me, not even a year after being in the hospital. There wasn't anything I could do about it. She'd follow me to the end of the universe.

"What are you thinking about," she asked softly.

"What kind of weapons Aasir can get us," I said. It was the best way to get my mind off Aayla. I couldn't stop thinking about her if I tried. And I figured to start the day off with something other than The Planner. However, that maniac wasn't number one on my to-kill list. That spot belonged to Abel, and he was back home in America, probably trying to sell the diamond. The only thing that put a halt to finding him was my mother coming to Africa with two monsters. Enjoy the little time you have left brother because soon, I'll be right back on your ass.

"Oh," Kim sat up in bed. "Why are you worrying about the weapons? Guns are guns anywhere you go. They all shoot bullets, right?"

153

I smiled at her. "Not even. Some shoot rockets, Rambolina."

She laughed and slapped me on the leg. "That was my first time shooting a grenade launcher. I didn't know I was gonna blow everything up. I looked up a video on how to use it."

"You almost killed us all, but it's all good," I said, hugging and kissing her cheek. "My baby came to the rescue."

"Whatever," Kim kissed me on the lips. "Are you hungry?"

"Yeah," I said. "I could go for some breakfast."

"Me too," she fell back on the bed. "Order some food."

"Cool," I called room service and placed a breakfast order. I got steak and eggs, and so did Kim. When the food arrived, I gave the waiter a hundred dollar tip, and he went nuts thanking me.

"Someone's generous," Kim said as I rolled the cart next to the bed.

"We got money," I said and prepared the food before sitting next to her. "I think we should share the wealth."

"You're a kind soul, Mr. Simmons," she said and smiled at me before looking at the food. "This looks delicious."

"It does," I cut a piece of steak. "And it's tender. Just the way I like it."

Kim took a bit first. "Um . . . amazing."

I took a bit of the steak, and Kim was right. The steak hit the spot. It was delicious.

"You mentioned the weapons," Kim swallowed her food. "Are there any particular weapons you're trying to get?"

I downed the food before I spoke. "We're gonna need some heat. If we run into the General, it's going down. He'll pay for what he did to Redd. The soldiers carry assault weapons, so we'll also need rifles. Maybe a few secondary handguns and a grenade."

"Do you know how to use a grenade," she asked.

"If you figured out how to use a grenade launcher," I said. "A grenade won't be that hard to handle. And yes, I do know how to use a grenade." I scooped a fork full of eggs into my mouth. They weren't the best but tasty. "The eggs are straight."

"They're dry," Kim said with a mouth full. "They could've done better." She got them down and said. "If we can get a rocket launcher, I want it."

"Look at you," I said, surprised. "Who are you tryna kill?"

Kim looked at me seriously and said. "Everyone."

28 – Abel

"There," Abel pointed to the location of the campsite from the back seat. "Just ahead, through the woods."

The two rebel soldiers Aayla ordered to help support Abel were in the front. Abel and Gina sat in the backseat of the Jeep. It didn't take them forty-five minutes to reach camp like it did while traveling on foot. They got back in fifteen minutes, and Abel still was worried about Snake. It would be hard to carry on the mission if anything happened to him. Snake skills were better than anyone he'd ever met. That's part of the reason they clicked. The General's army wouldn't hesitate to kill them if they suspected anything suspicious.

"Stop here," Abel told them. "We'll travel on foot and take them by surprise."

"How do you know if it's the army," Gina asked.

"Who else could it be," Abel countered.

The Jeep pulled to the side as Abel commanded. They spilled out of the vehicle, checked their weapons, and headed into the woods. Abel led the way to the campsite. They settled on the outer edge of the woods just out of view. It was early, and the sun was just beginning to rise. The trees provided excellent cover making it difficult to spot them.

"How do you want to handle this, sir," one of the soldiers asked.

Abel scanned the area for any other possible threats besides what was in front of his eyes. He counted three Libya soldiers. The soldiers were holding everyone at gunpoint except for Britt. She was nowhere in sight. Snake, Bam, and Silva were down on their knees. Sliva began to give the soldiers problems. He was resistant and wouldn't shut his mouth.

"Bumboclaat," Sliva shouted and stood.

Abel and the others watched as Silva tried to attack the soldier from the woods. Silva reached for the soldier's weapon and was hit in the mouth by his comrade. Silva fell to the ground, and the soldier he'd tried to disarm stood over him. The soldier pulled out a handgun and shot Silva three times in the head.

Suddenly, another soldier emerged from the plane, stood in the doorway, and shouted at the other soldiers before going back inside.

"You two," Abel looked at the rebels. "Take the left side, and we'll take the right. We'll deal with the guy in the plane last."

The soldiers set out through the woods and got in position. Abel and Gina maneuvered to the right. They had the three soldiers surrounded. Abel knew he had to move quickly before the soldiers decided to kill Snake and Bam.

"Ready," Abel asked Gina.

"Every second, baby," Gina responded.

Abel singled to the other side, and the rebels moved on the soldiers without being seen.

Snake saw what was happening and helped by distracting the soldiers.

"Stop moving," the soldier told Snake. "You want to die like your friend?"

By the time Snake could respond, Gina held her gun at the back of the soldier's head. "You first."

The soldier tried to react, but it was too late. Gina blew his brains all over Snake.

"Fuck," Snake said as fragments got on him.

The two rebels moved in fashion and wiped down the other two soldiers. One of the soldiers fell forward onto Bam.

"Dammit," he said, catching the soldier's weight. Bam fell over and pushed the lifeless body aside.

Abel crept toward the plane. He knew the gunfire would alert the soldier inside. His first thought was to prevent the soldier from bursting out of the plane and firing wildly at everyone. Abel was at the door when it opened. The soldier's eyes grew wide after seeing a man just as massive as the General. Abel pulled the trigger and shot the soldier twice in the stomach without breaking eye contact. Blood spilled from the soldier's mouth as he looked down at the damage. It wasn't over for him yet. The soldier went into shock, and rage kept him alive. The man in front of him would pay, but when he looked up. The barrel of Abel's gun aimed at his skull greeted him. His body fell backward into the plane. Abel heard a woman yelp after putting in work. He stepped inside and saw Britt. Her breasts were exposed, but luckily, she still had on shorts.

Britt saw Abel and ran over to him. She embraced him with a passionate hug. "You saved me!" She cried in his arms. Abel had made it just in time. The soldier had her dance slowly for him while removing her top. He enjoyed every moment while licking her breast and squeezing her ass. She was seconds away from being raped if Abel didn't intervene.

Abel didn't realize he had his arms around her when he said. "You're welcome."

Britt looked deeply into Abel's eyes. She wanted him badly. Abel had already captured her heart and now saved her from

159

what would've been a life-long torment. He was the man of her dreams. She visualized Abel penetrating her, kissing her neck, and licking between her legs. It was a fantasy that would soon come true. She decided to make a move. It was the perfect time while staring into each other's eyes. His lips called to her, and she went for a kiss.

BOOM!

Britt's head exploded while she was still in Abel's arms. Abel didn't budge. It was like he wasn't affected by a headless corpse in his grasp. He felt blood splatter onto his face as he let Britt's body drop to the ground. Gina's smoking gun was the only thing in view.

"Fucking bitch," Gina growled at Britt's dead body.

Abel looked at Gina and said. "You got blood on my face."

"I like you better that way," Gina sounded sarcastic. "It'll keep the sluts away."

29 – Jordan

Jordan couldn't believe what had happened to him. *Rick,* he thought. *You slick sonovabitch.* He saw the smirk on Rick's face off to the side. Rick had the balls to push him in front of the rebel, putting his life in danger. The barrel of the rebel's gun was pressed against Jordan's nose.

In most cases, people in this predicament would be terrified, but not Jordan. This was a piece of action to feed The Planner. It was feeding time. His mind shifted from calm and collective to downright ruthless. It wouldn't end well for the rebel.

"Get down," the rebel shouted at Jordan.

Jordan didn't move. Instead, he kept his eyes locked with the rebel. There was nothing more fascinating than knowing when a man was terrified of you. Jordan smiled at the rebel and moved forward, pressing his nose against the barrel to force the rebel backward.

The rebel couldn't match Jordan's cold stare, which frightened him. Something about the man in front of him wasn't ordinary. He'd beaten, tortured, and killed men before. This wasn't new to him. He could sense that the man at the end of his gun wasn't afraid to die. "You want to die!"

"Of course I do," Jordan grabbed the gun barrel and moved to the side. His swift reflexes scared the rebel, and he shot the ground. He snatched the weapon from the rebel and tossed it. The gunfire had to alert the other soldier. Rick would have to deal with him. Jordan focused on the rebel. He didn't need to use his weapon to take him out. He slowly moved forward as the rebel backed away with his hands up. The terrified soldier tripped and fell on his back, and Jordan jumped on him. He picked up a large stone and held it over his head.

"No," the rebel cried as the stone came down.

Jordan crushed the rebel's skull. He closed his eyes and sighed. "Ah," he felt pain in his ribs. The second guard kicked him off his comrade. Jordan quickly got on his feet as the rebel checked the dead body. He wrapped his arms around the rebel's neck and used his weight to fall to the ground, holding the soldier in a deadly chokehold.

"Ah . . .," the soldier grunted, trying to pry Jordan's arm from his neck.

"See you in hell, motherfucker," Jordan spoke in the rebel's ear. The rebel began to gag, signifying the end was near. He held on a second longer until he heard the soldier croak. "That's it, baby." He released his hold, stood, and brushed off. He spotted Rick relaxing against the wall.

"Damn," Rick said. "You're good." He'd strapped the rebel's weapon around his shoulders and scanned the body for valuable items.

Jordan stared at Rick for a long moment before laughing. "I'm gonna kill you but not now." He searched the rebel before stripping off his clothes. "Put these on." Jordan tossed Rick the clothes. "He was fat enough."

Rick caught the attire. "I'm good."

"Do you want to end up like those guys," Jordan pointed up the wall for Rick to see.

"What the fuck," Rick noticed four heads on spikes. "Since you put it that way." Rick dressed in the rebel's clothes, and they were a nice fit. Jordan had the clothes off the first guard by the time he was done.

"We need to move," Jordan said. "They'll come wandering when someone notices the guards aren't at their posts."

The two former partners made their way back to the plane.

Jordan was the first to approach and wondered why Adrian didn't meet him at the nose. Indeed, he was somewhere on guard. They were in rebel clothing which would make things suspicious, especially with a killer like Black Water.

"Welcome back," Adrian opened the door as the two men approached. He'd slipped because his mind was on getting some ass. Usually, he would've spotted a target before they were at the door.

"What the fuck is going on," Jordan stepped inside not before pushing the clothes against Adrian's chest. "Why are you inside the plane? This isn't like you."

Rick followed Jordan inside and spotted Noti sitting in her usual seat. "Are you okay?"

Noti saw a worried expression on Rick's face. "I'm alive. How about you?"

"If I wanted you dead," Adrian told Jordan. "You would be. A white guy wearing rebel gear is a bit obvious. Don't you think?"

"It's dark," Jordan countered.

"Same," Rick answered. "I'm still kickin'."

"You run into a bit of fun," Adrian began to analyze Jordan and Rick.

"I'm surprised you can tell," Jordan said. He handed Adrian a rifle. "We were attacked because of him."

"Don't blame it on me," Rick snarled. "You wanted a fight, so you got one."

"Mind your business, rook," Jordan got in Rick's face. The two men were nose to nose.

"You remember what happened the last time you got in my face," Rick growled.

"Something's wrong with my memory," Jordan said. "Why don't you remind me?"

"We don't need this right now," Noti stepped between them.

"This doesn't concern you," Jordan shaved Noti out of the way.

"Don't put your hands on her," Adrian pushed the two men apart. "She's right."

Jordan stumbled back and took a fighting stance. He locked eyes with his brother. "Well, well, well, isn't this new. You let her get to you, little brother."

"Nonsense," Adrian didn't get in a stance. He just stood there with his arms crossed. "You two are fighting when we should be working together."

"Working together," Jordan laughed and looked at Rick. "You hear this guy? He's never worked with anyone in his life."

"They're both right," Rick answered after checking on Noti.

"We need to focus," Adrian spoke up. "Tell us what happened? Did you find any kerosene?"

Jordan spat on the floor. He was disgusted but loved being the outcast. They were against him, and that's how he liked it to be, against all odds. Something happened between Adrian and Noti. He felt it. Why else would he defend her after a shove? Her life wasn't in danger, and if it was, so what. Maybe they struck up a new deal while he was away? That had to be the case. *The rules have changed,* he thought. Jordan planned to kill Rick after the job was complete, but The Planner had everyone on his hit list, including Adrian.

Jordan stepped to the door and opened it. "Follow me."

30 – Kane

"Yo," I knocked on the door a second time. "You guys up?" I figured the boys were doing their thing all night. Someone had to be awake by now. It was nine-thirty in the morning. I put my ear to the door to see if I could hear anyone. I wondered if they even made it back. They could've stayed with the women. Nah, I shook the thought. Smoke is smarter than that. Ain't no way he's staying somewhere else in a foreign country. I banged on the door a lot louder. Good enough for everyone to think I'm the police. Finally, I heard someone approaching the door.

"Yo," I think it was Smoke's voice. "Chill, it's early. We didn't order room service."

This guy, I thought. "Bro, it's me. Open the door."

"Who's me," yep, it was Smoke. "I don't know any me."

"Nigga," I said, frustrated. "Open the door with your goofy ass."

I heard the lock turn and the door open. "Kane, my bad, bruh. What are you doing up so early?"

"We have to bounce," I told him. "Aasir will be here soon." I stepped inside and spotted Bruce on the couch, knocked out. He had the girl from last night wrapped in his arms.

"Damn," Smoke shut the door and walked into the kitchen. "I wouldn't have gotten fucked up last night if I'd known you'd slide through this early." He made a drink. "You want one?"

"Nah, I'm good." The bedroom door opened, and Bear walked out sleepily. "It's too early for me."

Smoke gulped the drink. "Helps if you have a hangover."

"Make one for me," Bear walked over. "Sup, dawg."

Bear gave me some dap. "Sup, playa. You ready to roll?"

"Hell, nah," Bear downed a shot Smoke handed over. "This early. Why?"

"You know what we gotta handle," I said, trying to be secretive in case the girls overheard our conversation. They don't need to be in our business.

"Fo' sho," Bear said. "You want me to clear house?" he looked at Smoke.

Smoke shrugged. "Fuck it, let's ride."

"Bet," I said. "I'll meet you guys in the lobby in twenty minutes."

"Twenty minutes," Smoke said sarcastically. "I was tryna get some head real quick."

"Man," I sighed. "Thirty."

"Run it," Smoke smiled.

"A'ight then," I left their room and entered ours. "Kim," I called. "You ready, babe?"

I walked into the room, and she was still in bed. "What are you doing?"

Kim sat up and said. "Lying down."

"I thought you were getting ready," I walked around the bed. "The boys will be ready in thirty minutes."

"Thirty minutes, babe," she cried.

"Yeah," I said.

"But," she whined. "I was hoping to get some head."

Ain't this bout a bitch, I thought.

We were in the lobby thirty-five minutes later with the rest of the gang. Kim and I were late after I gave them hell about being on time. To them, five minutes is a lifetime. Especially when you're the one bitching. I knew we'd get an ear full of shit talk.

"Oh, here comes Mr. Thirty Minutes," Smoke joked.

"Get'em Smoke," Bear laughed.

"Mr. If you're five minutes early, you're late lookin' ass nigga," Smoke continued.

"Ha," Big Bruce chuckled. "Bruh."

169

"Smoke . . .," Bear said. "Get his ass."

"Oh, the sun rises on the left side of my head, lookin' ass nigga," Smoke used his hands to make an oversized dome shape around his head.

Everyone started laughing, including Kim. "Stop talking about my baby, Smoke."

"Wha . . .," Smoke looked at Kim.

"Get her, bruh . . .," Bear said.

"Don't do it," Bruce warned, shaking his head no.

"Oh . . .," Smoke started and saw the way Kim looked at him. "Man . . .."

"That's what I thought," Kim slapped Smoke in the back of his head. "C'mon, the cab is out front." She turned to lead the but not before she heard Smoke say to me.

"You're lucky your big sister stepped in," he whispered at me.

Bear and Big Bruce chuckled.

Kim caught Smoke behind the head again. "I heard that."

"Wha . . .," Smoke cried. "I didn't say anything."

I shook my head. "Man, you haven't learned."

We made our way outside to the taxi. Aasir was standing next to the vehicle waiting for us. When he realized we were approaching, he popped the hatch and helped with our bags.

"Thank you, Aasir," Kim handed over her bag and got inside the van.

170

"You're very welcome, ma'am," Aasir said kindly.

Bear and Bruce followed suit.

"Buddy, buddy," Smoke dapped Aasir.

"Smoke Doggy," Aasir said with an accent.

I shook my head at them. These fools.

"About last night," Smoke said coolly.

"Bump, bump," Aasir said.

"Bump, bump, dawg," Smoke laughed, and they embraced. "Right on for showing us this place. It's some fine women around here."

"No problem, sir," Aasir smiled and held out his hand.

Smoke slapped it.

"No, sir," Aasir said.

"Wha," Smoke looked at me, and his eyes went back to Aasir. "You want a tip or something?"

"I gotta get that bread, sir," Aasir smiled. "Good service."

Smoke looked at me, confused. "You hear this guy?"

"He sent the girls last night, idiot," I assured him.

"Those were your hoes," Smoke asked, surprised.

"Indeed, sir," Aasir kept his hand out. "I have many jobs."

"Playa, Playa," Smoke reached in his pocket. "When we get back in town, I need to holla at the one with the long hair." He peeled five hundred off his backroll and gave it to Aasir.

171

"Thank you, sir," Aasir said. "You are more than kind. I will have her ready for you."

"Bet," Smoke got in the vehicle.

"So," I said. "You're also a pimp?"

Aasir smiled at me and shrugged. "Is that what Americans call it?"

"Either that or you're a mac daddy," I said. "Anyway, you got everything in order with the guns?"

"Yes," Aasir shut the hatch. "My friend is waiting for us to arrive."

"Cool," I hopped in the whip next to Kim. Smoke sat in the front passenger's seat.

"What took you guys so long," Kim asked and eyed me.

"Aasir has everything in order with the guns," I said.

"Smoke seems to be really excited about them," she said sarcastically. "Smiling and giving each other dap."

"Yeah," I answered without eye contact. "Real excited. You know how those two are. Smoke told him about last night."

"Um," I saw Kim roll her eyes at me.

"What," I pulled her closer. "I wasn't paying attention to Smoke. You know I blocked all that shit out, baby." I bit her on the neck playfully.

"Stop," she pushed my forehead back.

"You know you don't want him to stop," Bear said.

"Be quiet, Bear," Kim said.

"It's true," Bear looked at Big Bruce. "She always gets like this when Kane does something wrong. But she'll get on our ass if we fuck up."

"That's her nigga," Bruce said. "He's knocking her back out."

Bear chuckled. "You stupid, dawg."

That shit was funny. Kim caught me smiling and pinched my hand. "I can't help it if I smile at something stupid."

We stopped twice on the way to the gunman. Smoke used the restroom on the side of the road and another time for Kim when passing a small town. I estimated an hour and a half before we reached our first destination. Aasir stopped the taxi in a town made of stone. It was nothing like where we had just left. Tripoli was far more advanced, and this was like the stone age. I couldn't believe what I was seeing. People actually created this place, and it wasn't that bad. The buildings were well built, and one dirt road ran through the city. I saw in Kim's eyes that she was fascinated by it.

Aasir blew the horn, and a skinny kid came running out of the building to our right. The kid spoke to Aasir in Arabic, so I couldn't understand anything they said. When the kid ran back into the building, I asked Aasir was everything all good.

"We're straight," I asked from the back seat.

"It's fine, sir," Aasir looked through the rearview at me. "He's letting the boss know we have arrived."

I sat back, waiting for something to shake. Nobody in the vehicle said a word. They were probably thinking the same as me. Wondering if we fucked ourselves crossed my mind. I've been through a lot of shit lately, so I wouldn't doubt if Aasir set us up. Put up a few Americans from the airport, show them a good time, they'll trust you, and wham, it's a wrap. On the other side of the fence, I'm just paranoid as fuck.

Kim tapped me on the shoulder to get my attention. "Wassup," I looked at her.

"Look," she pointed to the right.

"What the fuck," I muttered. I was lost in thought and didn't notice about ten children had run out and surrounded the car with guns. Not one looked older than thirteen. "Aasir, what the hell is going on, man?"

"Trust me," Aasir said calmy. "Everything is fine, sir."

"Bruh," Smoke spoke up. "What you mean trust you? These li'l niggas got guns aimed at the whip."

Bear scanned the scenery, "This doesn't look good, dawg."

"Fuckin' right it don't," Big Bruce commented.

"Baby," Kim said worriedly.

Aasir turned back and eyed me and said. "Get out."

31 – Abel

"So there's a change of plans," Snake asked.

Abel wiped off the last spec of blood from his face. "Yes, things have changed."

"We're not here to meet the General anymore," Bam said. "Because of some lady who claims to be your aunt. Meaning exchanging the diamond for money won't happen. We came here for nothing."

Abel got angry with Bam but contained his emotions. "Like I said. She is my aunt. I don't want to remind you again. The offer will put me in charge of the rebels. We'll be able to control weapons and drugs smuggled in and out of Africa. I will be the leader of seventy percent of underground operations."

"What does she want from you," Bam asked.

"Nothing," Abel searched through his bag and found what he was looking for. "This is the key to everything."

"She doesn't want the diamond," Snake asked.

"No," Abel answered. "She has no use for it."

"Why can't we continue as planned, and you still become leader," Bam suggested. "Doesn't that work for the best?"

"No," Gina cut in. "Aayla is testing Abel's loyalty. The General is her enemy."

Bam gave Gina a look as if who asked you, bitch. He was pissed she murdered Britt. Britt was supposed to be his future wife.

Snake sighed. "She did provide soldiers along with transportation. I'm on your side, friend. Even if it doesn't end well." His emotions were all over the place. Gina blew Britt's head off right in front of his face. The little time he had with Britt was special. At least to him, it'd been special. She had the perfect body. Britt was shaped how a woman was supposed to look in his mind.

Abel looked at Bam. "She will lead us to Jar's headquarters. You will receive payment as planned. I'll hold on to the diamond for leverage against the General."

"Why didn't you say that initially," Bam muttered. He didn't care about anything other than his payment. The money meant everything to him, and under that came killing Gina.

"Shut your big mouth and listen next time," Gina said with her hands on her hips.

176

"I'm sick of your shit," Bam exploded and ran toward Gina. "I ought to —"

Gina swiftly aimed her gun at Bam's dick, stopping him in his tracks. "You ought to what, tough guy?"

Bam froze. He didn't speak or bother to move his eyes. He thought any movement would cause Gina to shoot off his balls. The bitch caught him slipping, and he hated himself for the mistake.

"Gina," Abel called from behind. "Haven't you done enough shooting for today?"

Gina stared into Bam's eyes for five hard seconds before smiling in his face. "You're right," She pulled the trigger, and the sound drove Bam crazy. "Bam," she joked.

"Holy shit," Bam reached for his crotch to make everything was still attached. The sound of the gun clicking told him he wouldn't have children. He began to cry.

"That's a surprise," Gina pulled back her gun. "I forgot to reload." She knew beforehand there weren't any bullets left in the weapon after putting in work. She used the last round on Britt. She noticed tears streaming down Bam's face. "Aw, poor baby. How about that milk?"

Snake watched what happened. He thought Gina was fucking coco for Cocoa Puffs. She was a female version of Billy the Kid. She terrified the hell out of him.

177

Bam's knees began to shake. He thought it was the end of the line. Gina would take him out before he killed her. If he'd eaten, he would've shit himself.

Gina walked over to her bag and picked it up. "Don't worry. I got it." She casually strolled to the Jeep, tossed the bag in the back, and got in the vehicle.

The two soldiers witnessed what happened between Gina and Bam. Both of them had wide eyes. They haven't seen a woman this ruthless since Aalya. The rebels thought Aalya was one of a kind.

Abel walked over to Bam. "C'mon, don't let them see you weak."

Bam didn't respond to Abel. He was grateful his dick wasn't lying on the ground.

Abel patted Bam on the back. "Get your stuff." He turned to Snake. "We have a place to stay. Don't worry about the tents. Leave them. Grab your belongings and get in the vehicle."

Snake nodded at Abel and watched him get in the Jeep. Bam was still in shock, standing there as if Medusa had turned him into stone. *Fuck me,* he thought. *Gina is on a rampage, and Abel isn't doing anything about her behavior. She's having her way with Bam. I could be next.*

Abel could be the rebels' leader with a maniac girlfriend. As long as Gina was by Abel's side, Snake planned to take his share and get far away.

32 – Kane

"Don't worry," I told Kim. "Everything will be all right. Just do what he says." The children surrounded the Taxi. Each of them had an assault rifle aimed at the vehicle. Everyone in the crew had a weapon on them.

I looked at each crew member and nodded to do as Aasir instructed. I was the first to move. "Ok, I'm getting out." I didn't know if the kid with the gun on me understood what I had said. The window was up, so it could've been hard to hear me. Either way, he didn't respond. I put my hand on the handle and opened the door slowly. Kim followed behind me, Bear, and then Bruce. Smoke was out of the vehicle on the opposite side because he sat in the passenger's seat. I kept my hands up where they could see them, letting them know I wasn't a threat.

Kim stood next to me and said. "They all look so young." She spoke low enough for only me to hear.

"Trust me," I whispered back, trying to be discreet. "They won't act like it." My eyes traveled over to Aasir. He was out of the vehicle with his hands high. That made me think maybe he was on our side. Although, it could be part of the plan.

We towered over the children, and it wasn't hard to notice who the men were. As a matter of fact, I take that back. They had the weapons. We weren't in any position to act brave. Any one of them could let loose, and it'd be over for everyone. I imagine they all had a full clip. Please don't make any sudden moves, I prayed. Hopefully, nobody would make a stupid move that would get us killed. I didn't expect them to, but you shouldn't assume anything. Stupid shit happens.

After about a minute or two, someone else came from the same building as the children. The man was short and skinny. No taller than five-eight and maybe around one-forty soaking wet. You could tell by the guy's clothes that he was the boss. He had on a black Doo-Rag, which I thought was a classic fashion statement. Also, a fishnet tank top, army fatigue pants, Timberland boots, two gold chains, and a Nike wristband on his left arm. Dark shades covered his eyes.

He walked up to me out of all people and smiled. "You want to buy my guns?"

I immediately noticed the bottom of his teeth was all gold. "That's right," It surprised me how good his English was after speaking.

"You pay cash," Unless you take debit, I thought. "American money." I kept my eyes on him the entire time.

"Good," he caressed his beard. It was clear something was on his mind. He scanned my crew. "Follow me inside. Only you. The others get in the taxi."

"Ok," I agreed.

"I'm coming with him," Kim eyed the man.

"Kim," I said worriedly. "Get in the taxi, baby. I got this."

"No," she refused. "I want to see the weapons for myself. No deal if he goes in alone."

The Man had a stone facial expression. There was no telling what he thought about Kim's demand.

Five seconds later, the mood changed. A smile replaced the grimace on his face. "She belongs to you?"

"That's right," Kim answered. "And we're purchasing together. Is there a problem?"

At this point, the deal could be over, and shit could hit the fan. I prepared for anything to happen. Kim was straightforward about how things would take place.

The man faced Kim. "I like you. Let's do business."

Kim and I followed the man into the stone building while the others waited inside the taxi. Whoever designed the place had good craftmanship. The walls were perfect. The floor was surprisingly level, and I noticed several African paintings on the ceiling. The one that intrigued me the most was a man squaring off with a lion. The detail put in the artwork was astonishing. I couldn't believe someone got up there and painted it.

We walked through the main area into a backroom. Three tables full of weapons jumped out at us. There were rifles aligned on each wall, corner to corner. I saw shit you wouldn't imagine in here. A fucking parachute, I thought. There was a section of the room with car parts. I guess my mans don't only sell weapons.

"Tell me what you like," the man said. He held out his arms.

There were a few things on my list I had to grab. Hopefully, things don't go the way they did when Smoke and I tried to purchase weapons from the kid. Sadly, Smoke put the guy down. A part of me was glad he was in the van. I need this transaction to go smoothly.

Kim stepped away, "I see something I like."

"Cool," I said. The man stayed close to me while I looked around. I picked up a Glock and scanned over it. "How much for this?"

"Five hundred," he said.

"Five," I said and looked at him. "Damn." I sat that bitch down and pointed to the Aks. "What about them?"

"Two thousand apiece," he said and crossed his arms.

"Shit expensive," I muttered.

"You are in Africa," he said. "Weapons like these are hard to come by. The prices are lower if you buy bulk."

I found everything I wanted before I asked for another price. "Five AKs, five Glocks, ten grenades, five vests, and five blades." I spotted something else that could be useful. "Let me get five of these flashlights attachments. Ok, what's the number?"

He thought about it for a second before he said. "Eight thousand, that's the best I can do."

Before I could answer, Kim broke in. "Add this to the list."

I should've known. Kim held up a grenade launcher. It was the same one she used at the police impound.

"It's exactly the same," she awed. "I love this thing."

"Those are five thousand," he said.

"All give you ten for everything," I said. "Work with me."

He stroked his beard for a moment. "Deal."

I pulled out a bundle of cash and tossed it to him. It was 10k exactly. The band the bank secured it with was still holding it together.

He fanned the money. "Smells good." He put the cash away. "Who are you going to war with?"

"No one," I said. "I just like guns."

He chuckled. "No one just like guns in Africa. You know, you remind me of a man I worked with a long time ago."

"Oh yeah," I was packing the weapons in a bag. "Who dat?"

"His name was Jar," he said. "The Lord of War."

33 – Jordan

Jordan stayed in front of the pack as he led the way to town. His mind wasn't on the kerosene. It swam around the idea of Noti and Adrian working out a new deal. He thought of different ways to torture them if they betrayed him. The Planner wouldn't show any sympathy to anyone.

Jordan looked back and saw Rick walking next to Noti. A grimace formed on his face watching the two as though everything was fine. Keeping Rick alive was now in his best interest. After all, they were partners. Rick couldn't trust anyone. He wasn't supposed to be here in the first place. His time should've been short-lived. *I have to get that asshole on my side,* he thought.

Jordan stopped and looked ahead where he was held captive. "Here we are."

Adrian stood next to Jordan. "How many?"

"Who knows," Jordan sighed. "We're in Africa. Motherfuckers will crawl from under rocks."

"Where is the kerosene located," Adrian didn't care how many men there were. Jordan was being a dick, and it wasn't hard to tell. It wasn't the time or place to start something, so he decided to leave it alone.

"Just over the right side of the wall," Jordan said. "A little ways down."

Adrian looked upward at the guard post above the wall. No one was in sight. The left side was also unoccupied. "I don't see anyone on guard."

"That's because you're wearing his clothes," Jordan responded. "I finished three on the way out."

"They didn't replace the two-tower guards," Adrian said. "Meaning their numbers are less than ten."

"You're right," Rick stepped closer. He wanted to know what Adrian had on his mind. He couldn't get left out of the loop this time around. "When we first entered the city, ten or so men attacked us. We took out three."

"I took out three," Jordan corrected. "You didn't do a damn thing."

"This isn't the time," Noti interrupted. "Let's get the kerosene and leave this place. It shouldn't be that hard."

187

"Of course," Jordan said with sarcasm. You could see it on his face. "These guys are amateurs. A bunch of idiots with guns."

"Those are the worse kind," Noti said while focusing her attention down the wall. "Which one of you has a plan?"

"We'll travel down the same path we did on the way out," Rick spoke confidently.

"Are you sure they won't be beyond the wall where you jumped," Adrian asked and looked at Rick.

"I'm with Rick on this," Jordan said. He didn't like the plan. The rebels could be where they were held, but it wouldn't matter because that's where the kerosene was located. This was the first step toward gaining Rick's trust. A simple agreement can go a long way.

"Alright then," Adrian checked his weapon. "Let's move."

Noti began to proceed, and Adrain stopped her. "What are you doing?"

"It isn't safe for you," Adrian told her with his arm out. "You should stay back and keep watch. If things get rough, I won't be able to protect you."

What is going on? Jordan thought, *so he's her protector now?* He saw the look in Adrian's eyes, and it wasn't the kind of look you give someone you didn't care about. This was more than business.

"What if someone catches me alone," she asked. "Then what?"

"Scream," Jordan said. "We might make it back in time."

"If I die, all of this will be for nothing," Noti said. "You'll leave here without a dime."

It didn't take long for Adrian to remember why he originally came to Africa. "Then I don't have a choice. Stay close to me and don't make a sound." He handed Noti his handgun. "Take this, and don't shoot it unless you're in danger."

Jordan hissed and shook his head. *Good, now she can shoot me in the back.*

Noti looked it over, "Ok."

"Lead the way, Cap," Jordan saluted Rick.

Rick knew Jordan was being a dick, but it sounded better than rook. "Follow me."

They followed Rick down the path. It was clear. No one was in sight, and they didn't hear a sound over the wall when approaching the jump point.

Jordan listened closely to see if he could hear anything just over the wall.

"I don't hear anything," Rick said.

"Sound good to me," Adrian said. "I'll go first."

"Wait," Noti said, just before Adrian leaped the wall. "Be careful. I need you alive."

189

"Don't worry," Adrian smiled at her.

Odd exchange of words that only meant two things in Jordan's mind, they had a new deal or were lovers. He went with the first assumption.

Adrian looked over the wall before fully committing. After scanning the area, he turned back and said. "Clear."

Jordan crouched to give Rick a boost. "Let's not do this again."

Rick didn't argue and took Jordan's help. He wondered why Jordan was being kind for a change.

Before Jordan leaped over the wall, he turned to Noti and said, "You don't wanna tell me to be careful?"

"Monsters like you don't die," she said.

Jordan smiled, latched on the edge of the wall, and pulled himself up. "Just remember, I'm not the only monster here."

34 – Kane

"You knew Jar," I stopped packing the weapons. "What do you know about him?"

"You want to know about the Lord of War," the man asked. "That's gonna cost you."

"What do you want," I asked while walking up to him. I stood next to the shorter man, looking down at him. I didn't wish to give him the wrong impression, so I held a friendly face.

"Friendship," he answered seriously.

"Friendship," I repeated.

Kim walked over and stood next to me. She still had the rocket launcher in her grip. "Baby, we need to get rockets. I'm gonna need at least five." She said evenly with her eyes on the weapon. When she realized I was in a standoff with Doo-Rag, she asked. "Am I missing something?"

"Nah, baby," I kept my eyes on Doo-Rag when I spoke. "We're all good. Get however many rockets you need."

191

"In Africa," Doo-Rag continued. "Friendships are worth more than money. If you want to stay alive. You will need friends. I'm a single man with children who have nothing. They work for me to feed their families. I take them in, train them, feed them, and teach them how to kill a man. They're better off with me than their mothers. They will grow into soldiers one day, and my army will be strong. You can't be a leader without connections. You come to Africa only to buy weapons when you can buy them on your land. Your war is here, and I want to help, son of Jar."

"Wait," Kim had a stunned expression. "He knew your father?"

I was shocked by what Doo-Rag said. He called me the son of Jar. Is it that obvious I'm his son? I wondered if he knew about Abel. Did this man work for my father? How many others are there that know about my father? There were so many questions that crossed my mind. I felt like everything hit me at once. Even though I wanted answers, I needed one question answered that was more important than the others. "Why is my friendship important to you?"

Doo-Rag smiled, showing off his bottom row of gold teeth. "You're here to pick up where your father left off. I want to be a part of your rise."

"A part of his rise," Kim interrupted. "What are you talking about?"

"You think I'm here to take over the weapons trade," I asked. "Become the new Lord of War?"

"I knew Bill Right had a son," he said. "His most trusted allies knew about his family. He made it his business to protect them if something happened to him . . . his sons, wife, business, and friendships. I knew you would come one-day seeking answers. Outside, I saw the look in your eyes, and it was the same determination I saw in your fathers when he told me he'd rule the smuggling business. At first, I thought he was a crazy man, but he started to prosper. I was his first employee. If you don't believe me, take a look for yourself." Doo-Rag pointed to an old picture framed on the wall that I overlooked before he brought it to my attention.

I stood in front of a photo of my father, Doo-Rag, and . . . my mother. My eyes began to sting because I didn't blink for the next two minutes. Seeing something like this shouldn't have surprised me, but it did. Doo-Rag looked like he was my age in the photo. He started young, a little older than the children running with him. I couldn't believe my father recruited a teenage boy to help with smuggling weapons. What was he thinking, I thought.

"Are you surprised?" Doo-Rag spoke over my shoulder.

I slowly shook my head while keeping my eyes on the picture. "Nah."

"Kane," Kim walked over and stood next to me. "Let's not keep the others waiting. You know how the boys get."

I sighed. "You're right. We have to go." I turned around and faced Doo-Rag and held out my hand. "You have my friendship under one condition."

"Speak," he said.

"Take me to my father's headquarters," I said. "I know it's in Mizdah."

"No problem," Doo-Rag shook my hand. "I should warn you now before we start our journey."

"Warn me about what," I said, strapping the duffle bag over my shoulder.

"What is it," Kim asked.

"First," Doo-Rag held up a finger. "You will need more weapons than what you have."

"Listen," I said. "This will be enough for what we're here for."

Doo-Rag laughed. "Don't worry. We are friends now. I won't charge for the weapons. I'll carry them in the truck to Mizdah. The General's army made your father's headquarters a campsite. It won't be easy to get inside without shedding blood. The General won't appreciate you on our land."

194

"Because of what happened in America," I said. "His men murdered my friend. We're not here for war, but we can be."

"I'm sure this is worse," he said. "The rebels raided the General's campsites. Word is he's out for blood."

"What does that have to do with me," I asked curiously.

"You have a lot to do with it," Doo-Rag walked over to the picture on the wall and faced it while he spoke. "You see . . . the Queen is the cause of the raids. She is the one in control of the rebel army. She's wicked and will burn your soul to get what she wants. The General will soon find her and murder her bloodline for the crimes."

"The woman in the photo is the Queen," I said. "My mother."

"The woman in the photo is not your mother," Doo-Rag turned around to face me. He took off his shades, and I saw his eyes for the first time. His left eye was gone.

Before Doo-Rag could answer, Kim spoke up. "Aayla."

"The same woman who took my eye," Doo-Rag put on his shades. "Queen Aayla."

35 – Abel

The ride back to Aayla's office was completely silent. Nobody uttered a word. The soldiers sat in the front seats. Abel and Gina sat together in the second row. Snake and Bam rode in the bed of the truck with the luggage. Snake was tempted to speak to Bam about his issues with Gina. Gina used to be an introvert before linking with the crew. When Abel first introduced Gina, Snake knew she was brilliant, and he saw something inside her that could benefit their cause. That all changed when she got involved with Abel intimately. It wasn't hard to notice the two had a thing for each other. He could also hear Gina moaning throughout the night when she visited their dorm room. After the museum heist failed, Gina went off the deep end. She'd turned into a ruthless individual that had a lust for violence. Gina gained an edge to her persona that he didn't see coming. He wanted to warn Bam to stop beefing with her, or he'd end up like Britt.

The Jeep came to a stop in the back of the building. Snake was still a bit suspicious about Aayla claiming to be Abel's aunt. He knew about Abel's parents, twin brother, friends, and girlfriends. They had been very close since meeting at Yale. They were almost inseparable until Gina stepped on the scene. He plugged into his mind to research the mysterious woman by digging up information over the web. There wasn't anything he couldn't find on the internet. The web was his second home and his place of peace. Ali showed him a few tricks that would come in handy. One of those skills involved scanning the international criminal database for terrorist intel. And that's what Snake thought Aayla was . . . a terrorist.

Abel got out of the truck and stepped in front of the bed. Snake tossed him his bag. Abel strapped it over his shoulder and looked at Snake. "I know you're worried. Don't be. This will turn out good for us, my friend."

Snake wanted to hide how he felt about Aayla. "I trusted you with everything we've been through. I'm not switching up now. Where else would I go," he smiled and held out his arms. "We're in Africa."

Abel grabbed his hand and helped Snake out of the truck. "You know, if there's anything you need to say, I'm listening. We started this together, and we'll finish together."

"No worries," Snake grabbed his bag out of the truck's bed. "Let's meet your aunt."

Bam hopped over and grabbed his bag. He watched the soldiers walk to the back door and knock. He sighed and spotted Gina eyeing him. He couldn't keep eye contact with her and turned away. She terrified him. He began to think he'd bit off more than he could chew. Abel and Gina were one. If he has a problem with Gina, there's one with Abel. They would die for one another. Soon he would have to figure out how to deal with them. He considered Abel a friend, and taking out Gina would interfere with their relationship. "This is the place, huh?"

Abel stood next to Bam and watched the soldiers walking into the building. "This is it." He turned to Bam and placed a hand on his shoulder. "I'm glad to see everything is alright. Aayla will take us to the warehouse. Nothing has changed. I won't forget to compensate you for your work. Trust me. Everything is in line. We're just using a better approach toward our goal."

"I trust you, Abel," Bam knew he had to lie to keep breathing. If Abel sense any disloyalty. It wouldn't end well for him. "I lost it back there. Please forgive me for my mistake?"

"All is well," Abel whispered. "I know Gina can be a bitch." He winked at Bam. "Stay cool, friend. Let's meet my aunt." Abel led the way into the building. Bam's job was far from done, and Abel needed clarification that his head was in a suitable space.

"Welcome," Aayla greeted everyone as they walked past the threshold.

Abel stood next to Aayla and introduced his company. "That's Snake and Bam. They're good friends of mine from school. Both men are brilliant and trustworthy." He pointed to them as he announced their names. "This is my aunt, Aayla."

Snake was the first to acknowledge the beautiful woman. "Nice to meet you."

Bam smiled politely and said. "Thanks for sending help for us at the camp. Those soldiers would've finished us if they didn't arrive in the nick of time."

Aayla sized up the two newcomers. They were half the size of Abel. *Useless,* she thought. There wasn't a use for brains in Africa. Only the strongest survive. Not the smartest. Strength and power are the two things that matter. Brains aren't a strength if a trained soldier wants your head. He'll have it on a plate by noon. She smirked at the two without showing a sign of approval. Something on Abel's shirt caught her attention. "There's blood on your shirt."

"I'm ok," he said. "It belongs to someone else."

Snake didn't like how Aayla looked at them. It seemed as if she wasn't in favor of them being with Abel. Maybe if he appeared aggressive like the soldiers or were the size of Abel, perhaps her tone would've been more accepting. Snake

199

attended school at Yale, and his parents are wealthy. With that comes a different kind of man apart from one raised to be a warrior. Their way of thinking and mentality are not compatible. Although, neither would survive in the other's habitat. And Snake could smell danger all around him.

36 – Kane

I watched Doo-Rag's mini-army load into an armored van. They carried just about every type of weapon you'd need to fight an army. I didn't feel good about the children helping out in this situation. In all honesty, they're kids. The General's army, who are grown men trained to kill, would destroy them. What am I supposed to do at this point? I needed Doo-Rag's help, but I didn't want to get any kids killed on my behalf. As I watched the children load into the van, I could only think about what lay ahead.

"What's going on," Snake asked as I got into the taxi. "Wassup with them?"

"Crazy," I said what I thought summed up the past thirty minutes.

"Wassup," Bear focused on me. "Y'all were gone for a minute."

"Those kids look like they're about to get down," Big Bruce said while monitoring what was taking place.

"That's because they are," I replied.

"What," Smoke said. "Man . . . what happened in there?"

"A lot," I sighed.

"Speak, my guy," Smoke got impatient with me. "Say something?"

I held up a finger and turned my attention to Aasir. "Follow your boy to Mizdah. He has a spot there where we can get situated."

"Bruh," Smoke eyed me. "Now we're following him? And those li'l niggas ridin' too. We're about to get fucked up." Smoke leaned his head back on the seat and sighed. "Fuck."

"Chill," I told him. "Everything is under control."

"How," Big Bruce asked. "I'm not the smartest nigga, but going to war with kids ain't the move."

"Listen to what he has to say before judging," Kim spoke up as Aasir started the van.

"I haven't said a word," Bear looked at Kim. "Because I know how it is. I've watched a few documentaries on how kids their age are trained killers. Some suicidal . . . strapping bombs to themselves and running at niggas." He shook his head. "Shit crazy."

"I don't know about all that," I said. "They're on some other shit. You're talking about terrorists."

Bear gave me a sarcastic look with wide eyes as if I'm the one trippin'.

"Whatever nigga, anyway," I focused on the entire group. All eyes were on me. I even caught a glimpse of Aasir staring back at me through the rearview. "I don't know how to begin. I had a dream last night and . . . it was about my father's business here in Africa. He stuck up a deal with the General. My mother was also in the dream, along with her sister. Her name is Aayla. My father cheated with this woman. I thought it was all bullshit until I saw a picture of my father, Doo-Rag, and Aayla inside his place. She's very real."

"Nigga," Smoke said, shocked. "I gotta burn one."

"Wha . . .," Bear's mouth dropped.

"Am I missing something here," Bruce's eyes flickered between us confusingly.

"We didn't know Kane had an aunt until now," Kim answered. "His parents never spoke of her."

"Oh . . .," Bruce said. "Ok, gotcha. But let me get this straight. You dreamt about your aunt, and then a picture confirmed it?"

"What a fuckin' coincidence, right," I replied.

"Damn, dawg," I heard Bear mutter. "With mom's sister. That's wicked."

Smoke turned around in the seat and held out a bunt. "You wanna hit this shit first? I know you got some shit on your mind."

"I'm good," I said and finished telling them everything I thought about the situation plus what Doo-Rag laid on me. They didn't know what to say, and Bruce was half lost anyway. I couldn't expect him to be as shocked as the rest of the crew. My aunt was a surprise to us. We grew up together, and Kim spent a lot of time with my mother. My parents never mentioned anything about Aayla.

I had several things on my mind as we rode to Doo-Rag's spot in Mizdah. Everything seemed to fall in place. I hated that I found out about Aayla this way. I wished my parents had told me about her. Instead, they kept her a secret even though it was for a good reason. She's the queen of a rebel army. The way Doo-Rag explained it. It's the largest gorilla group in Africa which is fuckin' insane. My mother is here to claim my father's money. There isn't a doubt in my mind that's what she came to do. The Planner and Adrian work for her. What the fuck can I say when I know she needs help. I'm beginning to think those monsters she brought along are a good thing. And that's talking out the side of my mouth. No doubt, I felt fucked up about it, but now I don't. I'd plan to get at them. That's why I bought the weapons. Shit has changed since we first arrived. The General's beef with Aayla could mean death for all of us. He's out for blood for something I didn't have anything to do with. Fuck it. We can air it out, and I put that on my boy, Redd.

It took roughly an hour to arrive at the location. The scenery told me they get active out here. The majority of the buildings were destroyed. Abandoned vehicles lined down the road on every block. As we drove through the city, you could see homeless people living in poverty. It saddens me how children affected by the living conditions have to survive this way. They don't get the same chance as everyone else. It reminds me of how privileged we are back home. You don't see people struggling to this degree daily. When I see stuff like this, I just wanna help somehow. You can say I'm the guy who wants to save the world. If I could put their weight on my shoulders, I would. Deep down, my efforts wouldn't be enough. It hurts to say it, but nothing will change as long as there are evil people in the world like the General, Adrian, and The Planner. Shit will carry on, and I plan to address them personally.

37 – Jordan

"It's enough kerosene to fly around the world," Adrian said while keeping his eyes pinned on the barrels. "This is a smuggler landing zone."

"What are you talking about," Rick asked. He didn't know anything about international smuggling. He was curious to know what Adrian thought.

"He means there could be weapons in the warehouse," Jordan answered. "I didn't initially think about it that way. Escaping was more important at the time. The rebels use the kerosene to fuel the planes transporting goods in and out of the area."

"I don't see any planes around here," Rick searched the area. "Hell, I don't even see a landing zone."

Adrian shook his head. "You're a cop, right?"

"What are you suggesting," Rick asked. "That I'm stupid?"

Adrian shrugged.

Jordan took the opportunity to get Rick on his side. Adrian was making it easy for him. *Thanks, little brother,* he thought in his twisted mind. "You should know this, Rick. You were one of the best profilers at the training center." Jordan hoped throwing a positive comment out there would work toward their partnership. He smiled on the inside, thinking, *just like the good ol' days, baby.*

Rick thought about it. When he realized the long dirt road in the center of town, he felt stupid. *Of course, in and out. No one sticks around long enough to get caught. They're smugglers, and the rebels don't want the Libyan army in their business.*

"You know what we have to do," Adrian crept over to the shed and peeped around the corner. He checked for any signs of rebels.

Rick hurried over, and Jordan followed behind him.

"You wanna look for supplies," Rick said. They were on rebel territory. He wanted to get the barrel of kerosene and get out. Adrian had other plans. They had weapons but would need more.

"Seems like a good idea unless you're strong enough to lift a barrel over the wall," Adrian looked back at him. "We can deal with the rest of them while they're occupied."

Dammit, Rick thought. *That's right.* After getting on the plane with two dangerous men, his only thought was to make it back to America safely. He's been unable to think straight with everything that had taken place. Helping criminals raid a camp wasn't the position he'd thought to be in. One barrel of kerosene is a tremendous amount of weight, even for the three men. They would have to construct a rope and pull system, which wouldn't work without material. Adrian was right. They'd have to make it through the town undetected. "We need to know where these guys are hiding if we're gonna take them out."

"What do you suggest, Rick," Jordan said without any sarcasm in his voice. It was the perfect setup. Adrian's life would be on the line, so he wouldn't take any suggestions from Rick. Jordan wanted to create as much conflict between the two as possible. The Planner would have to take a back seat for now while the FBI agent went to work.

"What do you suggest, Adrian," Rick said without hesitation. "You're the expert."

You stupid piece of shit, Jordan thought. *Why couldn't you just answer the damn question?*

"They want us to think they're in the warehouse," Adrian said. "But . . . I'm beginning to think they got the drop on us."

"What . . .," Rick scanned the area. "How—"

"Shhh . . .," Adrian held up his hand. "They're watching."

"Where," Rick whispered.

"The window," Adrian signaled toward one of the small buildings on the lot.

"Another in the window over there," Jordan pointed out.

Rick spotted both soldiers in the windows. "If they know we're here, what ar—"

"Shhh . . .," Adrian shushed Rick again, trying to concentrate on the rebels. "They're waiting for others."

"Wha . . .," Rick kept talking regardless if Adrian shushed him. "It's only three of us."

"They don't know that," Jordan spoke up.

"I thought the uniforms would help," Rick said.

"Rick," Jordan looked at him seriously. "You're white with blonde hair. They'll spot you coming from a mile away."

"Then why—"

"Shhh . . .," Adrian cut Rick off a third time. "They're moving." Adrian pointed to another building to the left. "Get ready." He aimed his weapon. "Watched the right, Jordan. Rick, you got the left side, and I'll take the front."

"Wait," Rick said. "That looks like . . .."

"Noti," Jordan finished.

"They captured her," Adrian muttered. His blood began to boil. Something deep down in his soul told him he had to save her at any cost.

"She was just behind us," Rick said. "That can't be her."

209

"She's wearing the same clothes," Jordan pointed out. "It's her." He noticed Noti casually walking next to one of the soldiers down the road. As they came into view, he knew it was her for sure. It was confusing because she didn't look to be in any danger. "Strange."

"What," Rick asked.

"She's calm," Adrian spoke up, looking through his scope. "Must've betrayed us."

"She wouldn't do that," Rick replied.

"Don't forget she hired us," Jordan reminded him. "Who's to say she didn't upgrade."

Rick held his feelings together. Mrs. Simmons is the reason they're in Africa. How could he trust her when Jordan and Adrian are two of America's most wanted criminals.

Jordan heard Noti call out to them. "What she say?"

"Don't shoot," Rick said.

"That's not gonna happen," Jordan said and looked through the scope. The first thought that hit his mind was she switched sides. There wouldn't be any money for him. He felt stupid for trusting her.

"Come out," Noti said to them. "They won't harm you." She stopped in the middle of the road, and so did the rebel. His weapon remained strapped around his shoulder. "You're safe."

"What does she mean we're safe," Jordan growled. "They're gonna fucking shoot us once we're in view."

"I think she's telling the truth," Rick watched as Noti stood with the rebel. He wasn't a threat to her, so why would he be a threat to them? Maybe she convinced them to work with her?

"Don't move," Adrian ordered Rick.

"They know we're here," Rick moved into the open with his hands up. "Stay if you want." He stood and stepped cautiously in their direction, helping not to get his head blown off.

"Don't fuckin' . . .," Jordan reached for Rick, but it was too late. Rick had moved away from his grasp.

"Shit," Adrian muttered. He thought about leaping over the wall. Then shooting it out crossed his mind. Both options didn't play out well for them. "Ok."

"Adrian," Jordan watched his brother move toward the pack. "Sonovabitch." Jordan was the last to move. Rick and Adrian decided his fate. *How did I let this happen,* he thought before revealing himself. His weapon was ready. If he would die today, he'd do it with guns blazing. Noti would catch a bullet for sure. She was the one who convinced him to come to Africa. Then Rick, the man who ruined his career after the ambush at the warehouse. Adrian would be next before he's gone. That would be a satisfying death wish.

"What is going on," Rick spoke up after everyone stood around eyeing each other.

"If you betrayed us," Adrian gripped his weapon. He usually worked alone. This shouldn't have happened if he stuck to his rule.

Jordan didn't care if Noti switched sides. He was ready for a shootout. Another member of the rebel group caught his attention. It was the same man who struck Rick in the head. A group of soldiers came out and stood by his side.

The lieutenant of the unit walked over and faced Noti. "Queen Aayla. I didn't expect your arrival today. These men are with you?"

Noti turned away and eyed Rick, Jordan, and Adrian. They didn't know anything about her sister. While they were away, a rebel snuck behind her, catching her off guard. He was shocked when he saw her face and immediately thought she was Aayla. Noti went with it and thought if she convinced him, there was a possibility she could fool the other soldiers. She also realized her sister became a leader, not just any leader, queen of an army. "Yes, lieutenant. They're with me."

38 – Kane

We stopped in front of a building that seemed like it had gone through years of destruction. I got out of the van, followed by everyone else. Kim met me in the back of the vehicle first. She didn't say a word, but I saw the look on her face that told me she thought the same as me the trip over. Her sad expression hurt my heart, and I had to comfort her somehow. "I know it's fucked up what's going on here, but try not to think about it."

"How," she said. "It's hard seeing all those children living on the streets without anything to eat. You see this place? It's devastating."

I saw a tear stream down her cheek, and I wiped it away gently with my thumb. "Kim, you're stronger than me. I thought the same as you after traveling through this hellhole. We have to remain focused. No matter what we do won't change anything around here. I do wish there was something we could do. This shit is sad. Remember what we're here for, and don't let anything distract you. My mother needs us, and I need you to help me find her."

"Ok, baby," she wrapped her arms around me.

I hugged her, pulled back, and kissed her forehead. "Try not to kill one of us with that rocket launcher."

She smiled. "Stay outta the way."

I waited for Aasir to open the hatch. Everyone grabbed a bag. Kim and I had two. She carried her belongings and the rocket launcher. I had my belongings and the weapons bag.

Smoke walked around to the back and grabbed his stuff. "Hey, sis, let me carry that for you?" He held out his hand.

"Thank you," Kim handed Smoke the bag with her belongings.

"I was talking about that one," he pointed at the rocket launcher.

"No way," Kim smiled. "This thing is staying with me, big head."

"Ah man," Smoke cried. "I wanted to check it out. That bad boy is cold. You tore shit up at the police impound." Smoke turned to me. "You only copped one?"

"That's it," I replied.

"Damn, my guy," Smoke sighed. "I could've fucked some shit up."

214

"That's why I didn't buy two," I said. "Doo-Rag might've brought one. I don't know what they have over there. You might wanna ask while they're unloading."

"Bet," Smoke hurried over to help Doo-Rag and his crew.

"This place looks like World War III," Bear said while grabbing his bag.

"What does World War II look like," Bruce asked and grabbed his stuff.

"The same way you looked when I bet your ass in Madden," Bear countered.

I chuckled, and so did Kim.

"That was bullshit," Bruce said. "Lucky ass."

"What's Madden," Aasir asked with a perplexed facial expression.

"A game we get too emotional about," I replied.

"I have to try it," Aasir said. "Do you have it?"

"Nah," I said. "If I make it back to America. I'll send you a copy."

"Thank you, sir," Aasir shut the hatch.

"Not another one," Kim shook her head. "I'll meet you inside, baby."

"Ok," I told her. She followed the others into the building. "I'm gonna need you to stay. We'll need transportation back to

Tripoli." I pulled out a bankroll and handed it to him. "Here's two g's. I'll give you another three on the way back."

"Thank you, sir," Aasir put the money away. "I'm here for you."

I held out a handgun. "Take this in case shit gets wild. You're gonna need to protect yourself."

"Yes," Aasir looked the gun over. "Protect myself."

"Do you know how to use it?" I asked skeptically.

"Of course," he said. "Since I was a boy, I liked to watch James Bond."

I laughed. James Bond, I thought. "Tight." I left Aasir and walked over to Doo-Rag standing in front of the building. He was giving his crew of li'l killers instructions, telling each one their task for tonight. Who was to stand on guard, where, and shift change. When he finished with them, I said. "So this is the place?"

When the li'l soldiers departed, Doo-Rag turned to me and said. "This is where I met your father. I was a homeless kid trying to feed my family. He asked me if I wanted to make some money. I think he felt sorry for me. I wondered what he was doing in a place like this. He told me to visit the General. I didn't believe him until the General, and his army showed up. Your father was looking for a place to start his business. This was the first location he checked out. It turned out there were too many

216

homeless people to operate. Although, he chose me to work for him. I considered myself lucky. I took him and the General further down the road. At the time, it was nothing there but land. That is where your father built his headquarters. A year later, he came back for me. I became his first soldier. He put me in charge of watching the place when he wasn't in the country. I became his first soldier, and as time passed. I became a lieutenant."

"He's the reason you recruit soldiers at their age," I asked Doo-Rag as we began to walk up a flight of stairs.

"They're from here," Doo-Rag answered. "Like me. Your father believed in me as I believe in them. I'm giving them a chance to make it out and provide for their families. Some die trying, and they're ok with it. They understand they could wait around here to die all the same. Nothing will change if they stay. I help as many children as I can. They look at me as their savior." He stopped at the door, and before he walked inside, he said. "I thought your father was my savior, but it's you who will save us all."

I stood there as Doo-Rag vanished inside with the others. You will save us all, rang out In my head. How could I? And then it hit me. It was the reason Doo-Rag decided to come with me. Someone had to stand up and fight back. He saw it in my eyes when I arrived at his doorstep. The same determination he saw in my father's eyes. I thought it, and so did the others. We all said this place looked like it was hit with a nuclear bomb. I told Kim there's nothing we could do to change things here. I was dead wrong. The place is like this because of the General and his men. If we take out the General, there could be an opportunity to revive the area with food and supplies. Doo-Rag isn't able to operate while the General controls the area. I don't believe I'm anyone's savior, but I do believe in what's right. I take back what I said initially about being here only to save my mother. I felt the weight on my shoulders because I wanted to do something when I saw those homeless children dying for food. This is my chance to make a difference. I stepped through the door, thinking about how to lure the General to Mizdah.

39 – The General

The General opened the door to the tent and stepped outside. He took in the fresh air hitting his nose. The tent reeked of sweat and blood, and the atmosphere provided a new dose of energy. He pulled out a cigarette and sighed, thinking about the name Aayla. He heard the name before but couldn't quite put his finger where. What boggled his mind was a woman leading the rebels. She was responsible for raiding his camps. He couldn't come to terms with a woman challenging him. No woman in their right mind could lead a group of ruthless men unless she's from the pits of hell. *The devil sent a woman to terrorize me,* he thought. Mentioning the General brought fear in men all over Africa. His brother is president of South Africa and not as feared as him. He's the muscle and the executioner, and Aayla would meet both men.

Abrafo walked out of the tent, wiping blood off his hands with a rag. He tossed the filthy cloth on the ground and stood next to the General. "Light?"

The General put the cigarette in his mouth, and Abrafo lit it. He took and drag and blew out the smoke. "I need to find the woman."

"I will send a unit to the location the traitor gave me," Abrafo flicked the lighter shut and put it in his jacket pocket.

"I know the name," the General said. "We've met."

"A long time ago, I assume," Abrafo said. "Women can be dangerous if not treated right. And this one is the leader of a group of traitors."

"Are you implying I had an affair with this woman," the General asked and puffed on his cigarette.

"You lied in bed with many women," Abrafo said. "None gave me the impression of being capable of this crime. Whores don't become leaders. They die whores. This one is a soldier. Not a whore. She has influence over men, which allows her to lead them. Beauty doesn't mean anything on the battlefield."

"I don't want anyone to know about a woman leader," the General told him and led the way to the Jeep. "If the people find out a woman stands against me. They'll think we're weak. I want to see her head removed from her shoulders. End her bloodline. No one will carry her name."

"It will be done, General," Abrafo said and opened the door for his leader. He got in the vehicle on the opposite side.

When they settled inside the Jeep, the General reminded Abrafo about the unauthorized plane. "The soldiers we sent to the plane site made contact?"

"They have," Abrafo answered as the Jeep pulled away. "Four Americans. Nothing to bother ourselves with. They're no threat to us. Maybe drug traffickers. Our men will report back after gathering more information."

The General took one last puff of the cigarette and tossed it out of the window. "I need a detailed report on every campsite the rebels raided. I want a count on weapons, supplies, and soldiers. And if any of them saw the woman."

"It will be on your desk in the morning," Abrafo said as his phone rang. He didn't recognize the number. He answered the call just in case it was information on Aayla. What he heard on the other end shocked him. The news was more important the Aayla.

The General noticed the look on Abrafo face. He knew something had stunned the lieutenant. The information had to be of great value to shock Abrafo. "What is it, lieutenant?"

"General," Abrafo did something he'd never done before. He gulped as if he was scared to relay the information. What he was about to say could get him killed if misleading. "We have to go to Mizdah. There . . . Americans have the Black Diamond."

40 – Kane

"It's done," Doo-Rag said after hanging up the phone with the General's lieutenant. He walked over to the edge of the roof and looked over, taking in the view.

I followed behind him. We went to the rooftop for privacy and to get a signal for his burner phone. I watched Doo-Rag smash the phone and throw it off the roof. No one would be able to trace the call back to us. He knew a soldier in the South African army that owed him a favor for saving his life. That's how he got the lieutenant's number. Doo-Rag held on to the favor for the perfect time. I know how much the General cares about the diamond. He came to America to get it. The Planner hired me to steal it. I remember reading the diamond's history in a brochure. What I read was wrong. It didn't mention anything about blood, sweat, and tears. How many innocent people died over the rock. My friend was one of them. I needed a way to get the General to

Mizdah. He would come for the diamond through hell or high water.

What I'm doing is dangerous. Not only for my crew but also for my mother. Suppose I'm right about her. She's going to my father's headquarters. Doo-Rag said the General turned it into a campsite. Hopefully, she wouldn't try anything while it's guarded by the army. I don't want her to show up until the smoke clears. The worst thing that could happen is the General mistaking her for Aayla. Even though she's blood, he'll have something special planned for Aayla. My mother shouldn't have to take on her death. Hope for the best, plan for the worst, right? We'll set up for The Planner and Adrian when the camp is under our control. Eventually, they'll arrive, and we'll be ready.

"The General will arrive in a few hours," Doo-Rag sighed. "We should get ready while we're ahead. We'll go to the warehouse and take out the soldiers on guard to lessen their numbers. The General is never alone. The lieutenant will travel by his side along with the first army."

"First army," I muttered. "I fought them in America."

"Ten of the bravest and strongest soldiers in the army," Doo-Rag eyed me. "They'll be a challenge. The captain of the first army is a man named Abrafo. I heard stories about how he tortures his victims. Horrifying. He is the deadliest man in Africa. He is the man I spoke with on the phone."

Damn, I thought. Abrafo is gonna be extra pissed off.

Doo-Rag continued. "You need to speak your peace with your friends. It could be your last time seeing them alive." He walked off and turned back when he got to the door. "I'm glad you're here, son of Jar."

"It was my brother who murdered my father," I told him because his connection with my father was deep. I've learned enough about him to sure the information. I wanted him to know who was responsible for his death.

He smirked with a slight nod. "It seems your aunt and brother are the same."

I watched him vanish through the doorway. Abel and Aayla are the same, I thought. My brother and my mother's sister. I think I'll stop at one child if Kim and I have one. Our family record is fucked up with second siblings. Let's pray I don't find out my father has a secret brother who is also fucked up in the head. I sighed and walked through the exit.

There wasn't a door to walk through on the floor we were on. The entire area was open. The top level of the building was vacated. The setup was perfect for what we needed. A few chairs, tables, and a chalkboard came to use. The crew put weapons on the tables with the other supplies. The li'l rebels had a shit load of artillery. Some of the guns appeared to

225

outweigh a few of them. I tried to imagine how they were able to tote them around with ease. Practice, I guess.

"What happened on the roof," Kim asked when I approached.

"We made a call to the lieutenant," I told her. "They'll be at the warehouse in a few hours."

"Did you speak to him," she asked concernedly.

"Nah," I said. "Doo-Rag did all the talking. He sounds like a mean sonovabitch, though."

"What if your mother shows up," Kim crossed her arms over her chest. "We need to figure out a way to keep her safe if that happens."

"I thought about it," I said while looking at the guns. "There isn't a way to keep her safe. We'll have to pray she's nowhere near the warehouse when it goes down. Doo-Rag told me the General has a first army that travels everywhere he goes. They're a special group of killers. I had it out with them before. Expect them to be by his side."

"They were at the warehouse with the General," Kim put up the rocket launcher.

"Same crew," I said. "Hopefully, they won't remember my face. Probably won't matter anyway. They'll wreck shit when the General realizes I don't have the diamond."

Kim held up the weapon. "I'll be the one wrecking shit."

Bear and Bruce walked over and stood in front of the table. They looked as if they were ready to head back home. Bear carried over a Mac-10 with a drum on it. Bruce had a submachine gun I'd never seen before. It looked like an older model compared to the other weapons.

"What is that," I asked, and he held it out to me.

"A PPSH-41," Bruce answered. "Doo-Rag said it's a Russian machine gun with a high fire rate. They nickname it, Papasha, which means daddy."

"Right," Kim said sarcastically. "They would name a gun, daddy."

"Ayee . . .," Bruce replied coolly. "It wasn't me. I picked it because of the 71 round drum on this hoe. I'm not tryna die. I just met y'all."

"Damn," I said, amazed. "Seventy-one ain't no joke. You talkin' bout droppin' shit."

"There's another one sitting on the table over there," Bruce pointed to the weapon. "You better nab it before one of them li'l niggas."

"Bet," I said. "I'll pick it up."

"What's the plan when we get there," Bear asked. "We didn't get the weapons for show."

"I gotta get some pussy after this," Smoke walked over and stood next to Bruce. "And burn one."

227

"Smoke," Kim looked at him. "We didn't need to know that."

I saw Doo-Rag walk over to the chalkboard. "We're about to find out," I answered Bear's question and nodded in the direction of Doo-Rag.

It took Doo-Rag two minutes to sketch a layout of the warehouse on the board. We sat in silence until he finished. The place was rather large by the look of the drawing. I counted four different areas containing five rooms. Two sections had two rooms, another with one, and the fourth section was an open space. Doo-Rag labeled each section, control room, security room, office, and warehouse space. I knew where I had to be, and it was apparent. The office. It was the area with one room in it that I figured would be a safe room—the place my father would stash his money. The first area my mother would run to and search.

I wonder if the General or Doo-Rag knew about my father's stash. The General has to know something. He turned the place into a campsite. Why wouldn't he? I don't expect any money to be inside the safe, but my mother is unaware of the General's takeover. We're rich, and I still can't comprehend why she would risk her life for money. There has to be something I'm missing that's not mentioned in the black notebook that only my mother knows.

"Kane," Kim whispered and nudged me on the shoulder. "You're zoning out again. Are you ok?"

I probably missed half of Doo-Rag's instructions. Kim would have to fill me in later. I had other things on my mind that wasn't as important with the shape of things. What's done is done. "I'm good, baby. Do you think Doo-Rag knows about the safe?"

"Of course he does," Kim whispered. "He was a lieutenant for your father. He remembers the entire layout of the building. I know what you're thinking. What if he's setting us up? I thought about it when he decided to tag along. Money is the ruler of all evil. He'll kill his entire family for seven hundred million. We're here to find the warehouse so we can save your mother. We need help doing that. If he takes the money, then so be it. It's worth using his resources to get what we want." Kim looked at me and smiled. "If he tries to hurt you, I'll cut out his other eye."

41 – Abel

The crew loaded the supplies in the Jeeps and headed out. Aalya wanted to travel discreetly, so three vehicles full of soldiers took different routes to Mizdah. Abel, Aayla, Gina, and a soldier rode in one vehicle. Bam, and Snake, rode together with two other soldiers. The third vehicle carried four of Aayla's top-ranked soldiers.

Snake was furious he wasn't able to ride with his best friend. Aayla was trying to keep them separated. He could feel it in his bones. He didn't bother putting up a fight because of the seating order. He didn't want to ride with Aayla in the first place. The woman scared the hell out of him.

Bam had a sour look on his face for the entire trip. Aayla didn't bother him as much as she did Snake. The woman was domineering, but he figured that's why she was the leader. The only thing that mattered to him was getting paid.

"You know she's gonna kill us," Snake said to Bam. "If you didn't know already."

Bam turned to Snake and shook his head. "Why wait?"

"Why separate," Snake countered.

"You heard what she said," Bam sighed. "To stay off the General's radar. You have to move differently here in Africa, smart guy."

"You're right," Snake agreed. "I am the smart guy. That's why you can't see that your life is in danger."

"The only person I need to worry about is the bitch Gina," Bam hissed. "You saw what she did to me."

"You're telling me she's doing this because she wants Abel to take her place," Snake threw his arms up. "It's obvious she's using him. She wants what's in the safe."

"Abel won't let that happen," Bam said. "Neither will I."

"Listen to yourself. You sound like a fool, Bam," Snake spotted the rebel in the passenger's seat, eyeing him through the rearview mirror. He kept his voice down only for Bam to hear. "She has a fucking army. You nor Abel can stop her."

"Abel is the leader now," Bam shook his head. "Leave it alone. You're beginning to piss me off. I have enough shit on my plate."

Snake sucked his teeth and turned around to face the window. He needed to come up with a plan and fast. If he

231

couldn't convince Bam, Aayla meant trouble. He would ride this one out on his own. Making it out alive was going to be more than he bargained for. There was one opportunity left to shift things in his favor. It would take a miracle, but he had to take a chance on convincing Gina that Aayla wanted them dead.

The Jeep moved fast through a broken town in Mizdah. Abel took in the scenery from the backseat view. He spotted many homeless people wandering about with children. He didn't feel bad for any of them. It's the way life goes, and there was nothing anyone could do about it. Every piece of destruction reminded him of profit. Someone was making money off the weapons used to destroy the town. They were short on food and water, and it didn't bother him one bit. They were dirt swept under the rug in his mind.

They came to another slightly upgraded area from the previous location. The only difference was no people were in sight. The town was completely deserted and in the middle of nowhere. The Jeep stopped at the first building. Vehicles two and three showed up when he got out, arriving on time as planned. Everyone met in the front of the building with their weapons ready. Aayla stood in front of the pack, ready to give instructions.

"The plan is simple," Aayla addressed the crew. "There are four areas in the building. A control room, security room, office space, and warehouse space." She picked up a stick and drew the images in the dirt as she spoke. The General's men will be on guard here, here, and here. There will also be a member in each section. We don't want them to alert the General. You will attach a suppressor on your weapons."

One of the rebel's opened a bag and handed each person a silencer for a handgun and assault rifle.

"Leave no one alive," Aayla continued. "Die honorably. Speak of nothing. Stay with the group you traveled with. Group A will take the office space. Group B will take the security room, and C will take the control room. We will gather in the warehouse space when the sections are clear."

Snake was glad Aayla wouldn't be anywhere near him. Although, the General's men would try to kill him on sight. He screwed a silencer on his handgun and rifle. He noted to watch the rebels. Aayla could've ordered them to complete the deal. He nearly got sick thinking about every wanting to kill him. Any moment of uncertainty and it was off with his head.

Aayla pointed down the road. "At the edge of town, there are several warehouses. The warehouse we're looking for is located In the middle. The others are parking garages—nothing of value but the vehicles. Check your weapons and move out."

Abel turned to Gina, "Are you ready?"

"Yes, my love," she grabbed the sides of his face and kissed his lips. She wanted Aayla to see. *There's a woman Abel cares about more than you,* she thought.

Aayla pretended not to care, but she got furious on the inside. Abel showed a sign of weakness, and she didn't appreciate it. She wanted to shoot Gina in the head badly that she had to turn away to regain focus. Abel was in the same position she was years ago with Jar. She fell in love with a man who would betray her. His father was the last man she had ever loved.

I'd say she's not happy about that. Snake kept his thoughts to himself. He saw the look in Aayla's eyes when Gina kissed Abel. She didn't realize he was watching her. The woman had it out for them. Gina wasn't on the hit list before. She is now. Aayla acted as if it didn't bother her, but Snake knew it was a problem. Abel needed to know Aayla's true intentions, and Snake made it his number one priority to expose her.

Bam stood next to Snake. "Group B, we're headed to the security room with these two."

"That's what she said," Snake replied as the group began to move.

"Hey," he whispered. "You still think she wants to kill us, don't you?"

"It doesn't matter what I think," Snake focused ahead. "We're about to face an army. That's scary enough right now."

"Don't worry yourself," Bam told him. "We have a fucking army with us."

"You know," Snake sighed and looked at him. "I used to think you were smart."

"I used to think you were dumb," Bam said. "And I still do." He hurried ahead, leaving Snake with his last words.

"Asshole," Snake muttered.

"Halt," Aalya head up a fist.

Abel stopped, and so did everyone else. The warehouses were in view. He didn't see any guard towers or windows. *Cameras,* he thought. *The place has a security room.*

"This way," Aalya made sure everyone followed her trail. "There is a blind spot where we can enter the building closest to the security room. Group B, once inside, shut down the cameras immediately. Group C, the lights."

The two soldiers in Group B and C nodded.

Abel followed behind Aayla. He didn't expect the building to be this massive. It was at least half a football field. The other facilities were decent in size as well. Jar must've moved a ton of shipments daily. They stopped at a side door of the building. He watched Aayla pick the lock with ease. The woman was a master. Her eyes looked back at him while holding the doorknob. Abel began thinking about his family. *This is where it all began,* he thought. *Jar built this place from the ground up,*

235

and somewhere in an underground bunker is seven hundred million. He prepared to become the man his father couldn't be. The money would be his, and he still possessed the diamond. Aayla made him the leader of the largest rebel group in Africa. He would achieve goals far beyond Jar's reach. He imagined controlling the African government. He held the power at the tip of his fingers. America would fall next in line by sending cyber attacks to each of the fortune 500 hundred companies. Payment wouldn't be enough. He'd demand ownership.

42 – Kane

After three long hours, we booted up and left Doo-Rags hideout. It didn't take long to reach the next town. The buildings weren't destroyed, and I didn't see any homeless people wandering around. Actually, there wasn't anyone in sight. The place seemed deserted. I noticed three Jeeps parked in a row. That seemed odd because they were the only vehicles on the strip. Someone, maybe the General's men are nearby?

"You do you think those vehicles belong to," Kim asked as we got out of the van.

"Let's find out," I met the crew in the back of the vehicle.

"I know shit about to get hot," Smoke said, eyeing the Jeeps.

"Three of a kind," Bear said.

Doo-Rag and his crow got out of their vehicle and hurried over to us. "We have company."

"Yeah," I said sarcastically. "We noticed."

"These vehicles belong to the rebels," Doo-Rag informed us. "This is not good. We must hurry."

"The rebels," I said. "I thought the General turned this place into a campsite?"

Doo-Rag had a concerned look on his face. "The rebels are trying to raid the warehouse."

"I don't see any warehouse or rebels, my guy," Smoke said.

"There," Doo-Rag pointed down the road. "Several warehouses behind the last building. Hard to see from here because of the hill. The middle warehouse is the headquarters." Doo-Rag spoke something in his language to his crew and gave us his attention. "They will ruin our plan if we don't stop them."

"I don't see the problem," Kim said. "Let them kill each other, and we'll finish off the rest."

"You don't understand," Doo-Rag led the way toward the warehouses. "The rebels wouldn't come here unless they're with the Queen. This place is off-limits to them."

We approached the end of the block, and I spotted the warehouses. The place my father started his empire. The place I read about in the black notebook.

I heard Kim say, "Why was it off-limits? That seems crazy because they raided the other campsites."

"The Queen wanted to wait for the code," Doo-Rag stopped. "Someone has given it to her."

"She's after the safe," I muttered. She wants my father's money. But who could've given her the code? I was ready to ask Doo-Rag, but Kim took the words right outta my mouth.

"Who would give her the code," Kim asked.

"Jar used to carry a book with him everywhere," Doo-Rag replied, looking at us all. "The secret is in there. Whoever has it has the code."

"Wait, what," Kim had a perplexed expression on her face. "The black notebook?"

Doo-Rag shook his head yes.

"That's not possible," I step in. "She must've gotten the code from somewhere else."

Doo-Rag looked at me seriously and said. "You don't know your father."

Fuck, I thought. Doo-Rag was right. My father carried that damn book everywhere. He wouldn't give the code to anyone except my mother. I don't believe my mother gave the code to Aayla. What if Aayla found her? Shit, that wouldn't be good. That's the only way she could've gotten the code.

"Where is the book now," Doo-Rag asked.

"In Amorioa," I answered.

"With who," he asked.

"With . . .," it was hard for me to say his name. "Abel."

"Abel is here," Doo-Rag said. "He's the one."

"Abel doesn't know about Aayla," I said. "Our parents never mentioned her. No way it's him."

"Abel saw the map," Kim muttered and then spoke up. "He studied it and the notebook. And . . .," Kim locked eyes with me. "He has the diamond."

"He has the Black Diamond," Doo-Rag asked and snatched off his shades. "Who is this, Abel?"

"My twin brother," I said.

"The one you mentioned on the roof," Doo-Rag said. "The one who took my friend's life?"

"Yes," I said. "Him."

"I'm sorry," Doo-Rag said. "Your brother and Aayla are working together."

"Ah . . . shit," Smoke said. "This nigga in Africa."

"My dream," Bear said. "I told you. It's true."

"What are you talkin' bout," Bruce asked.

"Bear had a dream we were in Africa with Abel," I answered. "He was asleep at my father's desk when I woke him."

"And you thought he was trippin'," Smoke said. "You should've told me about that shit, Bear. I would've been on my detective shit."

"Don't make it worse," Kim eyed Smoke. "Ok, what's the backup plan?"

"There is a door with a blind spot on the right side of the building," Doo-Rag said. "We can get inside there without being detected."

"Ok," I said, gripping the weapon. "Let's move. We already wasted enough time."

"Move out," Doo-Rag ordered his crew.

The li'l soldiers split into two groups of five and worked toward the left and right sides of the warehouses.

"They're good," I asked.

"They will set C4 on the vehicles in the garages," Doo-Rag said. "Then attack anyone who tries to enter the building once we're inside."

"Sounds good," I shrugged.

Doo-Rag led the way to the side door. I watched him prepare to pick the lock, but all of a sudden, he froze.

"Wassup," Smoke asked. "You good, my guy?"

Doo-Rag looked back at us and said. "It's open." He cautiously pushed the door open.

I didn't know what to think when he pointed out the unlocked door. My mind journeyed back to the three rebel Jeeps. Queen Aayla knew about the blind spot. They beat us inside, and I wondered if Abel was with them. The notebook held the passcode to the safe, which I don't give a fuck about. Seven hundred million isn't worth my mother's life. However, Abel doesn't give a fuck about family. Thinking about Aayla and Abel together was terrifying. I haven't met my aunt, and I already know she's not to be fucked with. Hell, she could've done me a favor and killed Abel and took the book. Who knows, they're both vicious and would kill to get what they want. I came here to save my mother and got myself and the crew in some extra shit with the General, Aayla, and possibly Abel. It's hard to think positive when they're at your neck. On the bright side of things, it's over if I make it out alive. If not, it's a good day to die.

43 – Jordan

After the rebels put fuel in the plane, they were back in the air. Noti told the lieutenant that Jordan, Adrian, and Rick were high playing customers here to buy weapons. The lieutenant apologized to Rick for knocking him in the head and throwing them inside a holding shelter. He provided them with food, water, and kerosene. They ate while the rebels loaded the plane with weapons. They treated Noti like a queen because they feared what she would do to them. Aayla had earned respect from each man in the group. Their lives and their family members' lives were on the line. And no one wanted to lose an eye for speaking out of pocket.

Jordan had some new toys to play with. He held onto a PKM while speaking to Noti "I can't believe they fell for It." He smiled and strapped an ammo belt of 7.62 NATO rounds over his shoulder. "Really, I thought I'd have to kill you."

"Why didn't you tell us you had a sister when we arrived," Rick asked, working with an AR-15.

"She's not anyone's concern," Noti replied with a straight face. She wasn't excited like everyone else because of the new weapons. That's why she hired Jordan and Adrian to put in work. However, she sat back with a Glock 17 in her grip. Some protection is better than no protection.

"Oh," Rick said. "She's definitely everyone's concern. She's the leader of a rebel army. They were fucking terrified of you. That tells me she's a monster."

"It's a lot of monsters around here," Jordan muttered with his head down and eyes on the weapon. He couldn't wait to use it.

"I didn't know she was a leader of an army," Noti sighed. "It's been years since we spoke."

"I tried to dig up information on your family two years ago when your husba—" Rick saw the look in Noti's eyes and didn't want to hurt her by bringing up Jar. "Sorry."

"It's ok," Noti said.

"Who gives a shit about her dead husband," Jordan spoke up. "Grow some balls, Rick. The guy was a fucking criminal. He paid someone to erase your background after 1993. Rick is the best profiler at the bureau, and he couldn't find shit. Zero information on Aayla. There, I said it."

"You speak as if you're not a criminal," Noti responded.

"And you speak as if I won't fuckin' kill you if I don't get my fucking money," Jordan erupted. He needed to yell at someone. He had enough of everyone's shit. "Keep in mind what the rebels told us. The General turned your dead husband's headquarters into a fucking campsite."

"Stop yelling, idiot," Adrian said from the pilot's seat. "I need to hear if Air Control has us on their radar. Keep it up if you want us to get shot down."

Jordan looked at Adrian and snarled.

"Good thing about that is the General will probably kill you first for what happened at the warehouse," Rick looked at Jordan and smiled. "Unless you can pull a black diamond out of your ass."

"I already tried," Jordan replied. "I only found the shit that's on your breath."

"Stop it," Noti spoke up. "You two will get us killed if you keep at it."

"Queen Aayla has spoken," Jordan said with sarcasm. "Hail to the queen."

"Idiot," Rick muttered.

"We're here," Adrian spoke over his shoulder. "Prepare for landing."

Noti, Rick, and Jordan stayed in their seats until the plane landed on a dusty road in Mizdah. Adrian shut the plane down and popped his secret hatch with all of his personal weapons.

"What the hell," Jordan watched his brother dig into his stash of artillery. "Sonovabitch, you were holding out."

"I didn't have a use for this stuff until now," Adrian screwed a silencer on a PP7. He grabbed several throwing stars, flash grenades, and smoke bombs.

"Who the fuck are you supposed to be," Jordan eyed him.

Adrian finished grabbing his equipment. "Your worse fucking nightmare." He stepped off the plane and walked past Jordan.

"We'll see about that," Jordan muttered. He didn't need to get fancy to kill—aim and shoot. That's all you need in his mind.

Rick stepped next to Noti. "Someone's home."

"More rebels," Noti said. They were standing at the edge of town. Four parked vehicles were in front of her.

"Company," Jordan walked over and stood next to them.

"Rebels," Adrian told him.

"The Queen can handle it like last time," Jordan joked.

"Not this time," Noti said.

"Why not," Rick said.

"She wouldn't come here without them," Noti said and walked to the building in front of the vehicles.

"Wait a minute," Rick followed. "You think she's here?"

Noti didn't answer. She was busy searching the front door. She pulled back a piece of wood on the side panel and found the key. *Still here,* she thought.

"This doesn't look like any kind of headquarters," Jordan said. "And I thought the General made this a campsite? Lying sons of bitches."

"The headquarters is that way," she pointed down the road without looking. "We're taking an underground route to get inside."

"How long has that key been there," Rick asked.

"Thiry years," Noti answered, stepping inside.

"No one thought to check this place out," Adrian asked.

"My husband owns the town," she said. "He paid everyone to move out. The army would shoot any trespassers."

Jordan was last to walk inside the building. The inside hadn't been clean in a long time, and he noticed it immediately. Dust was on everything, and spider webs inhabited wall space and furniture. He used his hand to chop the cobb webs as he scanned the area.

"Here," Noti folded back a long rug in the backroom. "I need your help."

The men gathered around in the room with her.

"Now what," Jordan hissed, looking at an empty wooden floor.

247

Noti kept her eyes on the ground and said. "Pry it."

"For what," Jordan snapped.

"You want to get paid, don't you," Noti asked.

Adrian shot the floor with his PP7 and the floorboard loosened. "There, it's done."

"I came this far," Rick said. "I might as well work." He crouched and began pulling the board up.

Jordan crouched to help Rick with the floor. "Let me help, buddy." He still wanted Rick on his side. This was the endgame. Noti and Adrian could finish him once they had the money. He didn't forget how they've been acting friendly with one another. He couldn't wait to kill them. It's been on his mind since he got back to the plane.

With the floorboard removed, it revealed a steel door with a keypad. "We can't shoot that bad boy." Rick eyed the passage.

Noti crouched and placed her finger on the keypad. "Let me handle it from here." The keypad lit green and unlocked the door. She pulled the hatch.

"Fingerprint scan," Adrian said. "Nice."

"Smart," Rick said. "The numbers were decoys. What happens if someone tries to enter a code?"

"The building would explode," Noti said with a straight face and led the way down.

"Remind me to cut off her finger," Jordan smiled at Rick and stepped down behind Adrian.

Rick was the last to enter. He thought about not following the others. This was his chance to escape. He stood there for a long minute, and no one returned for him. It was like they forgot about him. He couldn't leave Noti even though she was the person in charge. Jordan or Adrian would kill her when the job was over. He was interested to see what Jar had hidden away. He followed into the passage.

"I knew you would come," Jordan said as Rick caught up from behind. "You couldn't help leaving her with us."

Rick didn't say a word.

"It's not me you have to worry about," Jordan said over his shoulder. "I'm not interested in killing women or kids. I just want my money, and I'm out of here. You and the dark knight can figure it out." He lied, trying to give Rick the impression of him as harmless.

Rick remained at the tail end of the party as they walked through a manmade tunnel for five minutes. They finally came to an open area. Rick stopped and stood there, stunned. He didn't blink booauoc he thought what was in front of him would vanish. In the center of the underground bunker laid a table full of gold bars.

Noti stood in front of the pack. She turned around and faced them. "Grab the cart and load the plane."

"Holy shit," Jordan muttered. He couldn't believe Noti came through on her promise. This was more than what he could wish for. He expected payment in dollar bills, not gold. The only problem was he'd still need Adrian to fly the plane. He didn't think about it until now. *Oh well,* he thought. *I'll just have to wait to kill him.* He shrugged it off, grabbed the cart, and loaded the first bar of gold.

44 – Kane

"Wait," I said, stopping Doo-Rag before he halfway opened the door. "I have an idea."

"What is it," Doo-Rag said, holding off with his hand still on the door.

I had a vision of the floorplan in my head. Our lives were in danger, and we weren't in the best position. "One, I don't hear anyone inside and judging how many vehicles we saw. I would say it's at least five to ten men. Two, the General's men are dead. Otherwise, there would be an alarm sounding off or some kind of commotion. I dealt with these guys before, and they're loud. I don't assume everyone is dead. Agreed?"

Everyone shook their heads yes.

"Ok," I continued "Let's set up in the warehouse space just ahead. Whoever's inside must be in the rooms. We'll guard every door until we're sure it's clear. We'll catch them slipping. No one should expect us."

"What about the General," Kim said. "Eventually, he'll show with the first army."

"Right," I said. "Doo-Rag's crew will sound off when they arrive. We'll deal with them then."

"Ready," Doo-Rag asked.

I looked at the crew, and they were prepared for a fight. I turned to Doo-Rag and nodded that we were ready. He pushed the door open cautiously and led the way inside. In front of us, the first thing I spotted lying on the ground was a body. It was a dead member of the General's army. I'm sure he won't be the only soldier we'd find in a puddle of blood.

The inside of the warehouse was massive. I couldn't believe the amount of open space. You'd think they'd load the place with supplies. There were a few boxes here and there, but not much. It didn't resemble a campsite to me. Then I realized why the soldiers were here, which was why Aayla didn't send her army. The General sent his men to guard the safe. He wants what's inside, just like everyone else. The seven hundred plus million was on everyone's mind.

I looked around the main warehouse space. The area didn't provide much cover in case a war broke out. Doo-Rag took cover behind a large beam in front of the control room. I signaled to my crew to find cover as well. Kim followed behind me. She wasn't gonna leave my side, and that's how I wanted it.

Bear and Bruce were posted in front of the security room. Smoke posted next to Doo-Rag behind another beam. They aimed their weapons at the doors and waited for movement. I continued walking toward the office space and hid behind a forklift with a dead soldier still in the seat. He fell forward with his head on the steering wheel. There was a wrapped skid of goods on the forks. The same kind of boxes that were throughout the warehouse.

Kim covered behind two pallets stacked high next to each other. She's small, so it provided enough cover for her. I looked at the bay door to my left. A soldier lay slumped against it. He sat in a puddle of blood that trailed off under the door. These guys didn't have a chance, I thought. While I patiently waited for someone to emerge from the office. I could only think about how the rebels got the drop on the dead soldiers and if Abel was with them. The area was clean of gun shells, and it didn't appear to be a shootout. The soldiers carried rifles, and I think they didn't get an opportunity to use them. Someone knew what they were doing, which said they cased the place.

Suddenly, all the lights in the warehouse shut off. We were sitting in dark silence. I couldn't see a thing. Kim was a few feet away, and I couldn't tell if she was there or not. "Kim," I whispered. "Don't use the flashlight." She knew what that meant and didn't have to respond. The light would put her in danger by giving up her location. Hopefully, the others would keep theirs off until further notice. They could know we're here and move in. Someone was in the control room and flipped the switch. Maybe they saw us on the security camera and communicated with the person in the control room. So given the information, both rooms were possibly occupied by rebels.

What the hell is going on, I thought. A minute passed, and still no activity, no sound or movement. I wanted to speak to Kim and make sure she was ok. She would've signaled if something was wrong, but I couldn't help but worry about her. My thoughts were interrupted when a dim light from the office lit the room. The safe, I thought. We were good and still off the radar. Whoever's there wouldn't give up their location unless they're crazy. Before I could act, several lights flashed on from the control and security rooms. They were using flashlight attachments on their weapons. I saw their movement through the windows. They were looking for something other than us, which was good.

At that point, I didn't know what to do but wait. That's when a loud explosion went off. Doo-Rag's crew, I thought. The General was here. "Don't move," I said to Kim. "Wait."

"Ok," Kim said.

The door to the control and security rooms opened. I saw rebels leave the rooms and hurry over to the bay doors. My crew didn't engage. The loading dock doors opened, and the rebels began firing. I spotted six rebels with rifles. The warehouse lit up with gunfire and light shining from outside through the doors. I could see enough to make out my crew. They were holding positions. Doo-Rag decided to move toward the control room, and Smoke covered his back. Bear and Bruce kept positions in front of the security room. I signaled to Kim that I was moving in on the office space. The rebels didn't notice as I crept passed with Kim behind me. The noise was loud enough to cover our footsteps. We made it to the door. We stood on opposite sides with our weapons ready. I thought it would be good not to look through the window to stay discreet. I put my hand on the knob and turned it. I pushed the door open without exposing myself. I peeked inside and who I saw took my breath away. The man who murdered my father stood in front of a large steel door. Abel hurried inside and closed the safe behind him.

45 – Abel

"Shutting off the lights," Snake radioed Abel before the entire warehouse became dark.

"Hold position until further notice," Abel told them. "Once we're inside the safe, we'll contact everyone for the next checkpoint."

Gina turned on a dim light that was only bright enough to illuminate a five-inch diameter. She put the light on Abel.

Abel pulled out the black notebook and held it under the light. After receiving the book from the camp, he didn't bother looking at the page numbers with the number of distractions. He opened the book for Gina and Aayla to see. They gathered around him as he flipped through the book, reading off the missing numbers. "Three, ten, eighteen, twenty-seven, thirty-three, forty-five, fifty-one," he came to the end of the book. "That's the code."

"You do the honors," Aayla said to Abel.

Gina held the light on the keypad on the wall next to the safe.

They were taken by surprise when an explosion erupted, coming from the left side of the building.

"You have to hurry," Aayla told Abel. "The General has arrived. Someone got away."

"We cleared the building," Abel stood in front of the keypad while speaking to Aayla. "No one was left alive."

"We can't worry about that now," Gina said.

"Snake and Bam are out there," Abel said. "I still need them." Bam wasn't that much of a concern. Although, Snake is his closest friend. He wanted him alive. Their minds are alike, and keeping Snake by his side would provide versatility after the takeover.

"Are you a leader?" Aayla was barely able to see Abel's eyes in the dark.

"Yes," Abel answered as gunfire rang throughout the warehouse.

"There will be sacrifices," Aayla replied. "A leader should know this. Your soldiers are prepared to die."

Abel sighed and punched in the code on the keypad. Green letters appeared across the tiny screen that read, open. He pulled the door handle back and revealed the inside. It was utterly dark, so he turned on the flashlight and aimed the rifle down the path.

257

Aayla turned to the soldier that was with them guarding the office door. "Clear a path."

The soldier left the door and hurried down the passage.

"Ok," Aayla said to Abel and Gina. "The soldier will spring any traps for us to pass safely."

"You two go in first," Abel said. "I will watch our tail."

"Are you sure," Gina said. "I don't want anything to happen to you."

"I will be fine," Abel told her. "I'm right behind you."

"I'll lead the way," Aayla offered and went inside.

Gina kissed Abel on the lips and took off behind Aayla.

Abel stood there for a moment, thinking about his friend and if he should help. Snake was of high importance. His inventions were magnificent. Abel thought about all the obstacles they went through together. The energy put into every debate and chess match between the two. *He could be dead by now,* Abel thought. Snake wasn't raised to be a soldier. Neither was he but possessed the skills to survive, unlike Snake. Abel thought back to what Abel said. A leader should know there will be sacrifices. That's what it takes to be a leader, and he wanted to be more than just a leader. He wanted to be King. *Goodbye, my friend,* he thought before entering the safe and closing the door.

Abel traveled down the path until he heard the others just ahead. The flashlight attached to the barrel of his rifle guided the way. He was surprised Jar didn't install any emergy lights leading down the path. He wondered how long it took to construct. After three minutes of walking, he reached an open area with the others. The soldier, Gina, and Aayla stood around an empty table. "What's going on?" Abel lowered his weapon when he realized it was safe.

"Someone beat us to the punch," Gina spoke up.

"What do you mean," Abel said, walking over. "That's not possible. I'm the only person with the code."

"What about Jar," Aayla said, looking her nephew in the eyes. "Do you think he moved it before he died?"

"Why would he," Abel replied. Jar had possibly outsmarted him. The money was gone, and the only for his newly found army to gain position was the Black Diamond—one of the reasons for coming to Africa in the first place. All wasn't lost just yet.

"Maybe he knew something would happen to him," Gina suggested. "Or he moved everything to a new headquarters?" She turned to Aayla. "Is there another place Jar could've made a larger profit than in Africa?"

"Asia, Russia," Aayla throughout there. "But those countries are more dangerous. Here, Jar had the General on his side. He was safe and could move freely."

"She's right," Abel looked down at the table and closed his eyes to think. There had to be a reason the money was gone. He thought back to the map in Jar's office at home. The image became clear in his mind. Libya was the beginning and end and tied in with the notebook. There wasn't anything else more apparent.

"You still have the diamond and the army," Aayla didn't want Abel to lose focus. The only way to take over her mother's throne was to have Abel step in as the army's leader. The money would've been nice, but her only purpose was to leave Africa entirely and finally claim her place as queen back home.

Abel realized something peculiar about the setting that became evident. "You understand that seven hundred million can't fit on this table. Also, this place doesn't have a ventilation system. The money would've molded sitting after a long period of time. Paper is hygroscopic, meaning that it readily absorbs moisture from the air. The humidity is high enough to bleed the ink and cause mildew. This table held something else, diamonds or even —"

Gina interrupted. "Bars of gold, which is storable in any condition."

Not only did Abel change Aayla's perspective about the importance of Jar's stash. He brought to her attention what Jar possibly hid in the bunker. *Bars of gold,* she thought. The gold

260

could be of great value to other countries in exchange for partnership. You could get further with gold than paper bills. "Where do we start?"

Gina noticed the ground had shoe prints that didn't belong to them. "There," she pointed to another passageway different from the one they entered. "The prints on the ground are fresh, leading through that passage. Look at the trail next to the prints."

"Wheel tracks," Aayla said. She crouched and touched the dirt. "Let's follow the path."

Abel led the way through the tunnel. He was on a mission, moving twice as fast as everyone else. Less than ten minutes later, he found the cart. He scanned the surroundings. *Ladder,* he thought. He aimed the weapon upward through an open hatch, leading into an area that appeared to be a room. He listened for movement. Abel held out his arm as the other approached, signaling them to be quiet. He strapped the rifle over his shoulder, unholstered a handgun, and then climbed up the ladder. He froze, reaching the opening. The sound of footsteps was loud enough to be inside the room above.

Gina put her weapon away and readied a handgun. She began to climb up behind Abel.

Abel heard a loud thud hit the floor. He decided to take a chance and peep his head out through the hatch. The room above was clear, and he pulled himself up. *What,* he thought. A single twin bed, table, and lamp. Nothing else was inside the room apart from a rug and the remains of the floorboard. He helped Gina up while keeping his weapon on the door.

Aayla and the soldier entered the room from the hatch. They waited patiently, ready for a fight.

Abel signaled to the soldier with a nod.

The soldier crept through the door and stopped.

Everything went silent as the soldier stood there in the open. Suddenly, his body fell backward onto the floor. Abel didn't hear any gunfire as he scanned the soldier's body. Several throwing stars poked out of the soldier's chest. Before he had a chance to react, smoke filled the room. They were vulnerable if they stayed in the room. He had to choose to die inside the room or outside the room. Abel pushed forward while firing his rifle in every direction. Gina and Aayla came out firing their weapons as well. Abel noticed they were back at the starting point when the smoke cleared where they originally parked. He could see the vehicles through the windows of the building. The barrel of his weapon scanned the area. No one was in sight. They were the only ones left inside.

"Right window," Gina pointed out, noticing a white and two black men dressed as rebels. They were wearing the same uniform as Aayla's men.

Aayla looked in the direction of Gina's call out. "Those are not my men."

What are they doing here? Abel thought for a second. The white and one of the black men were cops from America. He didn't recognize the other black man. They were loading something into a plane. Abel took off toward the entrance and slid to a stop by the door. A fourth person appeared from the plane and took his breath away. "Mother."

Aayla noticed the woman in the doorway of the plane. "Sister, you have returned." She aimed at Noti, fired, and smiled, watching her target hit the ground.

46 – Jordan

"Man," Rick said. "This shit is heavy." They moved fifty bars of gold onto the plane. Rick was responsible for bringing them up the ladder. "They have to be at least thirty pounds apiece."

Jordan took the bar from Rick and placed it on another cart. "Stop whining."

"I can't believe you two were partners," Adrian said. "That's the reason I work alone."

Rick passed another bar to Jordan. "He wasn't that bad at first."

"That's the nicest thing I've heard either of you say," Adrian picked up a bar from the cart and gave it to Rick.

"He brought me coffee every morning," Jordan thought back. "Do you know how hard it was pretending I liked it?"

Adrian laughed.

"I knew it was bad," Rick joked. "That's why I brought you a cup every chance I got."

Noti walked over and noticed the guys laughing as if they were friends. *Money makes the world go round,* she thought. Rick seemed to be enjoying himself even though he was engaging in criminal activity. "What a pleasure this is to see."

Jordan watched Noti approach the doorway. "Don't worry. I'm off the clock."

"Uh-huh," Noti looked at the table. "Almost done." She was in charge of watching the front door and Jordan. She looked down the hatch and saw Adrian. "How is it going down there?"

Adrian looked up at Noti and smiled, taking in her beauty. "Good. About twenty left."

After hearing the number of bars he had to bring up the ladder, Rick sighed.

Jordan saw how Noti and Adrian looked at one another. *Don't worry,* he thought. *I'll bury you two together.*

"I wanted to ask you," Noti said to Adrian. "Can the plane hold all that weight?"

"I hope so," Adrian replied. "Because we're not leaving—."

Adrian was interrupted by a loud explosion.

"What the fuck was that?" Jordan said aloud. The explosion was powerful enough to shake the passage. It felt similar to an earthquake. The table shook, causing a bar of gold to vibrate off it. Jordan tried to hold what he could in place. "Dammit."

Rick dropped the bar and held on to the ladder until it was over. "I don't think there's a volcano around here."

"If we want to get out of here alive," Noti said. "We have to speed up the process."

"Fifteen left," Adrian shouted. "Rick, switch places with me. I'll carry them up the ladder."

Shoulda been that way in the first place, Rick thought. He got off the ladder and switched places with Adrian. Rick began to hand Adrian the bars of gold. "This is more like it."

Adrian rushed the bars up the ladder and handed them off to Jordan. Jordan took the bars and loaded them onto the cart. Noti counted the bars as they came through the hatch. It took Adrian less than five minutes to get the remaining bars of gold up the ladder and into Jordan's hands. The job was complete. They had every single bar loaded onto the cart. Rick followed Adrian up the ladder after passing him the last bar. They were all standing inside the room around the cart of gold.

"Let's get this loaded into the plane," Noti said. She walked out of the room.

Rick followed Noti. He knew his time was up. Jordan and Adrian got what they wanted out of him. They had the gold in their possession. They didn't have a use for him any longer. He decided to leave the room while their mind was on moving the gold. They could've easily dropped him right then, tossed him down the hatch, and locked it. His next decision was to develop a plane that would keep him alive.

Jordan and Adrian began pushing the cart through the door when gunfire erupted.

"C'mon," Jordan said. "Move faster."

"Just push the damn cart and shut up," Adrian told him.

Jordan and Adrian got the cart to the plane. Noti was inside, making space for the last load. Rick stood in the doorway, waiting for the handoff. Jordan handed Rick the first bar when Noti popped her head in the doorway.

"Look," Noti noticed several vehicles. "The General has arrived. Did you close the hatch?"

"No," Rick said. "Does it matter?"

Noti looked at Adrian. "The safe room leads to the hatch. They could flank us from the building while we're loading. It's best to close off the entry."

"I got it," Adrian said and ran off, leaving Jordan and Rick to finish loading. He hurried through the building into the room. He put his hands on the hatch and saw a bar of gold lying at the bottom of the ladder. It was the one Rick dropped during the explosion. Rick forgot to pick it up. "I'm solo from here on out." He muttered and dropped down to retrieve the gold. Far off in the distance, he could hear footsteps running in his direction. They grew louder every second. He picked up the bar and shot up the ladder. He didn't bother shutting the hatch. Whoever it was running made it to the ladder fast and aimed their weapon upward. Adrian vanished before being spotted, ran out the door, and noticed the others were still loading the plane.

"Damn," Adrian had to do something to buy time. He sat the gold on the floor, flipped a table, and hid behind it. A minute later, he heard more than one person in the room. Suddenly, footsteps that weren't quiet enough for his ears moved into the main area. He got his throwing stars ready and without being seen . . . let them fly.

Adrian took cover after hitting his target. *Rebel soldier,* he thought. The soldier wore the same uniform. It wasn't the General's men. It was Aayla's men who infiltrated the warehouse. Noti's sister. The same woman the rebels thought Noti was before gifting them the kerosene and weapons.

Adrian held a smoke bomb in his hand, and when the soldier hit the floor, he tossed it. Smoke clouded the air, and he rushed from the building.

Rick saw Adrian running and said, "we have trouble."

Jordan looked at Rick and turned around. "Shit." He saw the building full of smoke and Adrian heading in their direction. They still had ten bars of gold to load before they could leave.

Adrian slid up next to them. "Aayla's men. They came through the hatch." He handed Rick the bar of gold and grabbed another from the table. They began scrambling to load it.

Noti thought she overheard someone say Aayla's name. She stopped what she was doing and stood in front of the door. "Did someone say Aay—" she felt a sting in her right leg, grabbed it, and fell to the ground.

Adrian hurried over and crouched next to her. He saw blood leaking from her leg. "It doesn't look bad." He helped Noti off the ground and carried her into the plane.

Noti spotted several people shooting at them from the building. She saw two terrifying individuals. *Abel and Aayla are together,* she thought as Adrian sat her down in a seat.

Jordan gave Rick the final bar of gold. He thought while aiming the PKM, *let's party motherfuckers.* He let the PKM rip on the building, returning a healthy amount of rounds. Shells flipped out from the chamber and piled on the ground next to his feet. He didn't take his finger off the trigger until the weapon overheated. The barrel of the massive gun turned red. "Fuck," he dropped the gun and pulled out two .50 caliber handguns.

After taking cover in the plane's doorway, Rick returned fire with his rifle. Vacating the scene crossed his mind. The only problem was leaving Noti injured with two dangerous men. On the other hand, how far would he get if he didn't travel on the plane? He took and chance and ducked off inside. He saw Adrian working on Noti. "Is she ok?"

"She'll be fine," Adrian responded. He tore a line of cloth and wrapped it around Noti's leg.

"It's crazy out there," Rick said. "We have to get out of here."

"Thank you," Noti said to Adrian when he finished tightening the cloth around her leg. "You need to pilot the plane to a safe location."

Adrian stood and looked Noti over. "Ok." He rushed to the front and got in the pilot's seat. He flicked on the operations switches to turn on the aircraft. "Prepare for takeoff," he shouted over his shoulder.

Jordan returned fire while backing up onto the plane. He didn't shut the door because what he had on his mind before the encounter hadn't changed. Jordan aimed his weapon at Rick.

Rick was looking at Noti when he felt steel pressed against his head. "It's time to take out the trash, huh?" The thought of Jordan blowing out his brains hit his nervous system.

"You're smarter than you look," Jordan said. "Get the fuck off the plane and take that bitch with you."

"What about our agreement," Noti asked.

"You should have known better than to trust this monster," Rick said.

The engine's sound and gunfire made it complicated for Adrian to hear. "What," he shouted over his shoulder.

"That's right," Jordan said. "I'm a monster." He aimed the second weapon at Noti. "You're lucky I don't kill you. Now get the fuck off."

Rick thought about taking Jordan on, but Noti stopped him.

"Don't," Noti grabbed his shoulder. "We'll leave in peace."

Jordan kept aim until pushing them through the exit and then shutting the door. He smiled at them through the window as the plane took off. "Bye," he waved and turned around. He sat in the seat by the door, sighed, and closed his eyes. He began to laugh wickedly. "I did it," he muttered. "I fuckin' did it." Jordan opened his eyes and looked at the gold. He reached for a bar, and suddenly, the plane began to spin out of control.

47 – Kane

I hurried over to the safe, put my hand on the handle, and turned. I pulled hard even though I knew it wouldn't open. Abel was long gone. I sighed and noticed a keypad next to the door. Doo-Rag said the passcode was linked to my father's black notebook. I didn't have a clue what the code could be, and I wanted to go after Abel.

Kim slid next to me. "Do you know the passcode?"

"I'm dead," I got frustrated, staring at the pad.

"Was it—"

"It was him," I interrupted Kim. I didn't want her to say Abel's name. It still hurts inside after what he did to her and my father. Abel isn't worthy of a mention. Just know I'm on his ass now that I know he's in Africa. It's insane to think about us all being in the same place at the same time.

"Try your birthday," Kim suggested.

"It's not that easy," I said. "We're not here for Abel. I'll catch him later. I need to deal with the General. Getting you and the others out safely is my only concern."

"What about your mother," she asked.

I led the way to the door as I spoke. "She won't show while it's hot even with The Planner and his brother." I stopped at the entrance to peep out into the warehouse. "They're not crazy enough to take on the General's army."

"But we are," Kim said. "We should have thought about that before coming here, babe."

"For you and my mother," I said, aiming out of the doorway. "I'll take on the world." I saw Bear and Big Bruce with two other men they held captive. Smoke and Doo-Rag were standing in the middle of the warehouse with his crew. The assault on the warehouse stopped. Although, I could hear the sound of gunfire in the distance.

I hurried over to my crew. "I know these two," I said, looking at the men on their knees.

Kim stood next to me. "Don't kill them just yet. I want to speak with them first. Maybe they'll be kind enough to tell us why they're here in exchange for their lives."

"Get with Doo-Rag and his crew," I told Bear and Bruce. "Finish securing the warehouse and search these two. Kim, come with me."

"Bet," Bear said.

"I got you," Bruce agreed.

Kim followed me out of the warehouse. Abel went into the safe, so there had to be another entrance that I wasn't aware of. We left through the garage doors cautiously. Bodies were all over the place—the General's men. Other soldiers were in the area, having it out with what I assume Abel's crew. We made it to the town safely, and the first thing I noticed was a fucking airplane.

"What the . . .," I saw a shocked look on Kim's face.

"Hey," I touched her shoulder. "You can stay with the crew where it's safe."

"It's ok," she said. "I can't let you go alone."

We stayed close to the building while moving forward. I saw the General and his army up ahead. They were retreating into their vehicles not far from the aircraft. That's when I saw a woman and a white man pushed out the plane's door. I stopped and looked through the rifle's scope to get a better view. "Mother."

"Kane," Kim grabbed my shoulder and shouted. "The Planner is getting away on the plane!"

"What," I lowered the weapon. "The Planner?"

"Yes," I saw him.

"You sure," I asked.

"Absolutely," she said with a serious look in her eyes.

"You know what to do," I said.

"Yes, baby," Kim crouched down, prepared the rocket launcher, and held it on her shoulder.

The plane shot by us all and caused the General's vehicles to swerve off course. I followed the plane with my eyes as it took to the air. "Babe . . .," I said, not wanting the plane to escape.

"Shh . . .," she said.

"Babe . . .," I said, ignoring her. "They're getting away."

"Quiet," she said right before a rocket soared through the air and hit the plane's tail.

I watched the aircraft spin out of control with the tail end on fire before disappearing. I thought to myself. Finally, The Planner is dead. The plane left a trail of smoke leading downward, so I knew it had crashed somewhere far off in the distance.

"No," I heard Kim shout.

I didn't know what she was worried about. She'd hit the plane, and my mother was safe. "You're good, babe. You killed The Planner."

"No, baby," she pointed up the road. "The General has your mother."

"Wha . . .," I looked through the scope. While I was paying attention to Kim shooting down the plane and watching it crash.

275

The General got back on course. I watched him and his men handle Rick, my mother, and two other women. His men tossed them into the back of a military truck. "Mother," I yelled and took flight.

I ran as fast as I could, trying to catch the General. The vehicles pulled away, leaving a cloud of dust behind. I heard Kim shouting my name, but my legs wouldn't stop moving. The only thing on my mind was saving my mother. I shot at the vehicles while running, but I couldn't hit anything. My aim was off, and when the weapon clicked, signifying I was out of ammo, I tossed the gun and kept running. I made it to the first building, where we parked our vehicles. "Mother," I shouted one last time, but she was gone. I started crying as I bent over, holding my knees to catch my breath, thinking I'd never see her again. The General would do horrible things to her. Things my mother wouldn't deserve. My chest heaved as I stood there, lost. And just when I thought things couldn't get worse, someone tackled me from the side.

48 – Jordan

"Oh . . . shit," Jordan said as the plane spun out of control. He held on to the seat to avoid getting thrown all over the place. The gold occupied his mind, and he didn't think to put on the seatbelt. Bars of gold crashed into the walls, the floorboard, one cracked a window, and another smacked his kneecap. "Holy fuck," Jordan cried, holding his knee. Twenty-six pounds of unexpected weight colliding with his knee hurt like a bitch.

Adrian gained some control of the plane. "Hang on. It's gonna be a rough landing." He steered the aircraft as best he could, trying to remain steady. He pulled back on the steering wheel to lift the nose of the plane. Their chance of survival was less than five percent. That was good enough for him. It would've been helpful if the gold wasn't weighing down the aircraft. *Open space,* he thought.

Jordan fell on the floor and sled to the cockpit. Several bars of gold followed behind and pounded on his body one after

277

another. He was getting a one-of-a-kind beatdown. He looked at Adrian while on his back. "Land this sonovabitch!"

Adrian didn't bother to look down at Jordan lying between the pilot seats. He kept his eyes focused ahead and hands on the controls. "Three, two, one," the plane crashed in an open field and slid to a rugged stop. Adrian leaned his head back on the seat rest and sighed. "Fuck."

Jordan lay on the floor. The landing knocked him out cold.

The plane got smoky, and Adrian decided it was time to move. In any other situation getting as many bars of gold off the plane would be a priority. Instead, he grabbed Jordan's legs, dragged him to the door, and opened it. He got off first after positioning his brother where he could pull him off the aircraft by his feet. He didn't see Noti or Rick but didn't have time to dwell on it.

"Don't say I never did anything for you," Adrian held Jordan by the ankles and pulled him off the plane. Jordan's head bounced off several steps but nothing that would kill him. When his body hit the ground, Adrian dragged him through the dirt a clear distance away from the plane. He fell backward onto the ground, exhausted.

Jordan slowly regained consciousness. He held the back of his head. "Ahh . . .." His vision was blurry for the first ten seconds. When the surrounding became clear, he panicked and swiftly got to his feet. He saw Adrian lying close by. "Adrian," he called, thinking his brother had died in the plane crash. The plane was in horrible condition, and he thought only The Planner could survive a wreck that devastating. That thought lasted until he heard Adrian speak up.

"I saved your life, you piece of shit," Adrian opened his eyes and sat up straight. "You owe me."

The thought of money made him think of the gold. "The gold bars. I'm fucked." Jordan kicked the dirt, looking at the destroyed aircraft. "All of that for nothing! I'm gonna kill whoever did this to me."

"Slow down, cowboy," Adrian stood. "If you're fine. The gold is fine. We'll have to find the bars in the rubble—no big deal. Although, I need an extra mill for saving your life, which . . . brings my total to four million and leaves you with one million."

Jordan scrunched his face. "What are you talking about, shit for brains? That's at least two hundred million in gold."

Adrian burst out laughing. "What? You idiot. What did she promise you? One bar of gold is worth roughly . . . sixty-three thousand US currency. We loaded eighty bars, dickhead. That's around five mill."

"Bullshit," Jordan retorted.

"She got you, dude," Adrian fell back onto the ground laughing. "She fuckin' got you."

279

Jordan watched Adrian laugh on his back with his back in the dirt. He thought about it for a moment. *He's fuckin' right. She got me.* Seeing the bars of gold for the first time excited him, and he'd lost train of thought. As a former FBI agent, he should have known the bar's worth. One hundred million in gold bars wouldn't fit in a jet. You'll need a cargo plane. His blood began to simmer, thinking about it.

"And the bad part is you threw her off the plane," Adrian laughed.

"Shut up," Jordan said calmy. "I have a new offer for you."

"Oh yeah," Adrian said. "Shoot."

Jordan turned to the plane and watched smoke come from the engine. He was surprised it hadn't blown already. "You help me find and kill her. You can take all the gold."

Adrian didn't want to make a decision he'd regret. Noti was more beautiful than any other woman he's met. He wanted her, and after what she did to him on the plane, he needed her. His job kept him from being with a woman long term and making time to find the perfect woman wouldn't happen if he continued. "Ok, I'll help." Adrian watched Jordan walk off. "Where are you going?"

"Hunting," it wasn't Jordan who spoke. It was The Planner.

49 – Abel

"Take cover," Abel yelled after seeing the American officer reveal a PKM. He held Gina close as they took cover. A vast array of bullets shattered the building's windows. Abel thought the assault would never end. He kept Gina covered as he yelled over to Aayla. "Listen for the reload."

Aayla shouted back. "On it." Noti had returned to Africa after leaving for America with the love of her life. She would pay for abandoning her for all those years. Aayla thought about what she would do to her sister if she saw her again. The shot to Noti's leg was just the beginning of what Aayla had in mind.

"Remind me to bring one of those next time," Gina said to Abel, fascinated by the heavy weapon. She prepared her gun for an attack while patiently waiting under Abel's arm.

After a whole minute, the weapon was finally out of ammo. "Now," Abel stood from cover and was the first to return fire. Aayla and Gina followed suit and put their guns to use. Abel watched the black and white officer retreat into the aircraft. He lowered his weapon when they were gone. "Halt," he signaled with a balled fist.

"I can't let her go," Aayla began to move, and Abel stopped her.

"Wait," Abel looked into her eyes. "You're making a mistake. They could be waiting for us. The man on the plane killed a soldier with throwing stars. He's more dangerous than all of us. Let's regroup and go from there. See what they do first."

Aayla sighed. Abel told her right. "Okay, let's regroup with the others and take the plane."

Gina was about to unload on the plane when she noticed the white officer and Noti getting pushed out of the door. "Look at what's going on." She got Abel's and Aayla's attention.

They stared at the aircraft and watched The Planner kick Rick and Noti off-board.

"It's like a dream come true," Aalya said, watching the white man support her sister from falling.

"He kicked them off the plan," Abel muttered to himself. His mother stood in the open with the white officer. Both were easy pickins. Things got sweater a few seconds later as the plane began to leave without them.

"She's mine," Aalya pulled out her handgun, thinking of shooting Noti in the head at close range.

"Don't kill her," Abel spoke up. "We need to know what was in the safe and where the plane is heading."

Aayla stopped. "Does it matter?"

"Yes," Abel said. "Let's find out what they know, and then she's yours. Gina will go with you, and I'll radio the others with further instructions."

Aayla smiled at her nephew, thinking how great a leader he'll be.

Abel watched Aayla and Gina go off to capture their prey. He touched his ear to radio the others as they left out the door. "Shit," he searched around on the ground. The earpiece had fallen out of his ear somewhere between running in the passage and shooting at the plane. He backtracked, tracing his steps back to the hatch. He dropped down and found the earpiece at the foot of the ladder. He popped it in and radioed Snake. "Snake, come in." He climbed up the ladder, waiting to hear from his friend. He spoke up after no response. "Snake, come in." Nothing came back through the receiver. Even the tracking device on his watch was green.

Abel was confused as he stepped back into the lobby of the building. Snake didn't respond, and he wondered if someone had taken his life. Abel had to shake the thought from his mind when he looked out of the window and saw Aayla and Gina in trouble. The General's men had tossed them along with Rick and Noti in a truck, taking them captive. He took off, and by the time he reached the door, the vehicles had pulled away. He leaned against the door frame, lost in thought, thinking about what just happened. The General captured Gina and Aayla.

"Mother," a familiar voice shouted.

Abel looked up and saw Kane bent over and holding his knees. He couldn't believe his brother was right there in front of him. *What is he doing here?* Abel was dealing with mixed emotions. Gina and Aalya were gone, Snake and Bam didn't respond, and the safe was empty. He had nothing and no one. He roared and bolted at Kane with one thing on his mind . . . kill.

50 – Kane

I fell hard to the ground. Dust got into my eyes, making it difficult to see who had attacked me. The person on top of me was massive. The guy had to be over two hundred pounds. I could barely breathe because he knocked the wind out of me. I held on for dear life when we fell to the ground. It was the only thing I could do to protect myself. I locked my arms around his waist, keeping him close until I had a chance to recover. The move prevented him from smashing my face. It was already hot out, and a few blows to the head from a man this large could mean the end.

He broke free after struggling with me for a few seconds. I couldn't hold on for long because he had incredible strength. I rolled out of the way just in case he tried to kick me while I was down. After getting into several fights, I learned that's what attackers do. I swiftly hopped into a full fighting stance. It didn't take long to realize who was standing in front of me. Abel.

285

"How did you know where to find me," Abel growled.

"I came here for mother," I responded.

"Bad decision," Abel kept our conversation short and rushed me again.

I braced for his attack. It wouldn't be the same outcome before when he snuck me like a hoe. I waited until he got in range and used his momentum to flip his ass over into a bodyslam.

"Ah . . .," Abel roared down on his back, and I noticed he grabbed his ribs.

"After I kill your bitch ass," I kicked Abel in the ribs, sending him into a frenzy. There wasn't a doubt in my mind that he was in an extreme amount of pain. I kicked him a second time. "Your friends and bitch gettin' put up." I meant every word I said. We captured both of Abel's boys, and the chick that rolls with them was out there somewhere. No worries, I won't forget her face after our run-in at the hospital.

"Ah . . .," Abel groaned, trying to roll out of the way.

I grabbed Abel by the leg. He flipped over and kicked me in the stomach. I ate that shit. There wasn't anything he could do that could hurt me. My father was on my mind. Thinking about how Abel brought himself to kill the man who raised us made my blood boil. Africa wasn't as hot as me. I sat down on Abel so he couldn't move, UFC style. One, two, three, four punches back to back bashed Abel's face. Every time I landed a blow, the back of his head collided with the ground and bounced back. "Bitch," I growled and continued to paint my fists with his blood. It felt good beating Abel to death.

"Kane," I heard Kim call my name from a distance.

I ignored her and kept pounding on Abel's face. He was gonna take this ass whipping before I kill him. He wasn't as sharp in this fight as in the last. It was Iron Mike Tyson vs. an amateur boxer. Pick one. It didn't matter. My anger hit an all-time high that I could've bit his fuckin' ear off. Either blood got in my eyes, or Abel's face was covered in it. I don't know how many times I hit him in the face, but he appeared to be dead. I knew he hadn't died because I felt his chest taking in small breaths of air.

"Kane," I heard Kim getting closer.

BOOM!

Suddenly, I felt a sting in my shoulder that hurt like a muthafucka. "Ah . . .," I roared and fell off Abel. I grabbed my arm and quickly got on my feet. The person standing with a gun aimed at my head was the second person on my to-kill list—The Planner.

"Look at what we have here," Jordan said with a demonic look in his eyes.

"You couldn't pick a better time to show your ugly face," I said sarcastically. I didn't realize the energy spent punishing Abel got me exhausted. My knuckles felt swollen as well.

". . .," Jordan smirked. "Where is your bitch of a mother?"

"Fuck you," I said and spat on the ground. I saw people spit on the ground in movies, so I knew it meant to disrespect someone in these situations.

"Oh, you're a tough guy," Jordan snarled. "I'm sure he'll tell me," he waved the gun in Abel's direction. "Goodbye, smartass."

"Don't you dare," Kim slid in with the rocket launcher aimed at Jordan. "I'll fuck up your whole day."

I saw The Planner sigh as if he was tired of the bullshit. "Please, you're not that dumb. You'll kill us all, you stupid bitc—"

He didn't get the word out. I knew Kim was with the shit, so I got on the move when he gave her his attention. I ran a few paces and dove out of the way. Luckily, The Planner wasn't all that close to us. Kim let that bitch rip because a loud explosion came next. "Ah . . .," I hit the ground and rolled over, got on my feet, and spotted Kim. My eyes went from her to The Planner. The sonovabitch made it. I saw his pistol raise while he was still on his back.

"You stupid bitch," he roared and started firing shots. "You fuckin' stupid bitch!"

I hurried over to Kim. I couldn't think about killing Abel or The Planner as bad as I wanted to. I shielded Kim with my body and pushed her back toward the warehouse. "Go."

Kim dropped the rocket launcher and took off down the road. "Kane," she cried.

"Don't worry about me," I shouted while ducking and running, trying not to get hit by one of The Planner's wild shots. "I'm right behind you!"

"My face," I heard The Planner shout. "Ah . . . you bitch!" More shots followed his cry.

We finally made it back safely.

I held Kim closely. "Are you ok, baby?"

"Still here," she said. "How about you, love?"

"I'm straight," I said and smiled. "You're out of your mind." She's smart enough to know I was referring to shooting a fuckin' rocket that could have ended our lives.

"I know," she said. "I could've killed us."

She kissed me passionately. "You know I'm getting some tonight. And I want breakfast in the mourning."

"Anything for you, baby," she kissed me again and grabbed my crotch. "Love ya."

"I love you too," I led the way into the warehouse. Smoke and the rest of the crew had everything under control.

"Glad to see y'all made it," Bear said, walking over with Smoke and Big Bruce.

"You doubted us," Kim said with a smile.

"Him," Bear smiled. "Not you."

"A'ight bet," I joked.

"My nigga," Smoke said. "I knew you'd pull through."

"Yeah," I said with an even face. "We're cool, but my mother is trouble."

"Wassup with Mom Dukes," Bear's facial expression turned serious.

"Man," I started. "The General took her."

"Nah," Bruce said. "Damn, bruh."

"Fuck," Smoke said. "How?"

"Shit got crazy," I started and explained what happened.

"So what's the move," Bear asked.

"I don't know yet," I said honestly. "Maybe Doo-Rag can hit the lieutenant again, and we can set something up."

"Baby," Kim said. "I don't think the General will come after what happened."

"You could be right," I said. "We still have to try."

"I have something for you that will get the General to bite," Bear said. "When I searched your boy over there." He pointed to Abel's boy. The taller one of the two. "I found this on him."

My eyes lit up when I saw what he had. "The diamond."

"We told him we had the diamond," Bear said. "Now we do."

51 – Sisters

Noti watched her son cry out as the vehicle sped off. *Kane,* she thought from the back of the truck. She closed her eyes and wondered if she'd ever see him again. She still had one more move up her sleeve. She sighed and opened her eyes and saw Aayla sitting across from her, locked in.

Aayla eyed her older sister but didn't say a word. There wasn't anything to talk about. Noti left her behind. What's done is done. Noti didn't try to contact her or their mother after she ran off. Noti left her with nothing. Aayla fought for everything she had. Their mother wouldn't let her return to Jamaica empty-handed. With Abel now in the picture, she could return home and become queen. She wasn't worried about the General. Abel has the diamond and would trade it for their lives. Gina, of course, would be a part of the deal.

Gina saw how the women were staring at each other as if fighting in their minds. Neither said a word or broke eye contact.

She wondered what happened between them to hate each other. If it weren't for the handcuffs, they would've fought to the death.

Rick saw the women eyeing each other but focused on the soldier riding with them. The soldier kept a straight face as if nothing bothered him. Rick would've made a move but decided it was too dangerous. He was smart enough to know the General wanted something from them because otherwise, they would've been dead.

They rode in silence for the next hour until reaching their final destination. The soldier riding in the bed with them hopped out. He released the latch, releasing the bed's door. He aimed his weapon at them, signing for them to exit. They stepped off one by one, guided into a building, and led to a prison cell. They each had a cell of their own.

Rick was pushed into his cell and turned around, angry. He backed off when he saw the barrel at the tip of his nose.

Aayla walked into her cell peacefully. She didn't take her eyes off Noti as she was forced into a cell next to Gina's.

Gina backed into her cell with her eyes on the soldier. She wanted to get a good image of him implanted in her mind. No doubt he was dead when she escaped. "Don't forget me."

Noti stood at the cell bars. "Get me the General."

"Shut up, woman," the soldier said.

"You would be wise to follow my order," Noti said calmly.

The soldier smiled and aimed between the cell. "Don't be stupid. The General will see you when he's ready."

Noti took a seat when the soldier left the holding area. She sighed and looked over at Aayla. "You missed."

Aayla chuckled. "No, sister." She stood and walked to the cell bars. "That shot wasn't meant to kill you, but the next one will."

"I knew you would come for me," Noti said.

"Then you're a fool for coming," Aayla told her.

"You were always one step behind, sister," Noti said. "Remember who showed you the way."

"You did nothing for me," Aayla shouted. "But run off with Jar! When I was left here alone to fight for my life, where were you? Mother took it out on me because you were her favorite. She thought it was my fault you left. It took years to convince her otherwise. I had to earn her respect. When she found out what happened, she gave me permission to kill you if you returned to Africa."

"You always were a fuckin' baby," Noti smiled.

"Words coming from a housewife," Aayla laughed. She may have been the little sister, but she was larger than Noti. She trained with rebel soldiers daily, workouts, running, and shooting. She was the perfect soldier and more deadly than most men in Africa. She didn't become the rebel leader by gaining the popular vote. She had to be a monster, and savagery propelled her into leadership.

Rick knew Aayla meant business, and seeing her for the first time didn't change his mind. Back at the camp, the rebels thought Noti was Aayla. Men feared her when she wasn't around. He'd never seen men more terrified by a woman than Aayla. "We need to think about working together to get out of here instead of fighting."

"Shut up, cop," Gina hissed.

Rick looked at Gina but didn't say anything.

"Mother will fall in love with Abel," Aayla said calmly. "He'll bargain the African Black Diamond for us. Then I'll take him home to meet mother before she dies. The General will release you to me as a bonus. I'll take my time killing you. Maybe I'll let you see mother pass the crown to me."

"Fuck," Rick muttered. *The General came to America for the diamond. If Aayla's telling the truth, we're fucked.*

"I came back to Africa for one thing," Noti began to elaborate. "In the Blood Diamond War, the General's father was killed protecting the diamond. Another man murdered that man and escaped with the dia—"

"The diamond," Aayla interrupted. "We know the story."

"Wrong sister," Noti corrected her. "Diamonds."

"You lie," Aayla said.

"I have the Pink and Blue African Diamonds," Noti laughed wickedly. "Now I know Abel has the last diamond. Thank you, sister."

"The General won't believe you," Aayla said angrily.

"The General will do anything for his precious diamond," Noti said. "I had him eating out of the palm of my hands when I told him I had the other two."

"You used us," Rick said, realizing what Noti had done. "Jordan, Adrian were pawns in your plan."

"Yes," Noti said. "You were a mistake. I never meant for you to come. I needed those fools to bring me to Africa undetected. The small payment of gold was to throw them off. I figured Abel was here for my husband's safe when I saw him from the plane. What other reason he'd be here after murdering my husband? I figured he had his black notebook. The rebels at the camp showed me Aayla's power. Abel and Aayla together crossed my mind." She paused and smiled at Aayla. "Two demons working together. I informed the General I could stop you from raiding the camps along with the diamonds. Your men were talkative, sister. You and two diamonds are worth five hundred million. You and three diamonds, one billion."

"Lies," Aayla exploded. "Why are you still in a cell?"

"Abrafo," Noti shouted.

Seconds later, Abrafo returned with the General. They walked over to Noti's cell, and he opened it.

Noti stepped out and eyed Aayla. "Always one step behind."

The General looked at Noti. "You have the diamonds?"

"Yes," Noti said and turned to Aalya. "When you see mother in hell, tell her I said hi." She left her sister with that and stopped at Gina's cell. "This one comes with me."

Abrafo stood firm and said. "Yes, Queen Noti."

Author Bio

King Coopa J was born December 24, 1983, in Indianapolis, Indiana. He began writing fiction while incarcerated in 2010. Reading street literature inspired him to become a writer. He also has a passion for reading mystery, thriller & suspense novels. Kane, his first book, was created after making a bet with an inmate that he could write a novel. He currently lives in Maryland with his two sons.

Check out all of my books on Amazon!

Made in the USA
Columbia, SC
05 June 2024

36693443R00181